'You don't remember me at all, do you?'

Saffi's jaw dropped in consternation. 'Remember you? Should I?'

No wonder his manner had seemed so strange. Her stomach was leaden. So much for a new beginning. Even here it seemed she had come face to face with her vulnerabilities.

'Have we met before?'

'Oh, yes. We have.'

Matt said it in a confident, firm voice and she floundered for a second or two, thrown on to the back foot. Of *course* there would be people here that she had known in the past...

'I was working in the trauma unit. But I definitely remember *you*. How could I forget?'

His glance moved over her face, taking in the soft blush of her cheeks and the shining hair that fell in a mass of soft curls around her face.

His eyes darkened, as though he was working through some unresolved torment. 'You still look the way you did four years ago.'

Dear Reader

I couldn't help wondering what it must be like to lose your memory and not know anyone around you. How would it be to forget the people you once loved—even perhaps someone you'd hoped you might one day marry?

How would that feel—for both people involved? And would that love stand the test of time? Maybe it's possible—but what if something has gone terribly wrong? Something that is now forgotten?

These were the emotions I wanted to explore when I wrote about Saffi and Matt.

Saffi faces a huge challenge after she is hurt in an accident, but fortunately Matt is there to lend a helping hand as she recovers. Will they manage to find their way to true love when there are so many pitfalls along the way?

I hope you enjoy reading their story.

With love

Joanna

A DOCTOR
TO REMEMBER

BY
JOANNA NEIL

Published in Great Britain 2014
by Mills & Boon, an imprint of Harlequin (UK) Limited,
Eton House, 18-24 Paradise Road, Richmond, Surrey, TW9 1SR

© 2014 Joanna Neil

ISBN: 978 0 263 24365 9

Harlequin (UK) Limited's policy is to use papers that are natural,
renewable and recyclable products and made from wood grown in
sustainable forests. The logging and manufacturing processes conform
to the legal environmental regulations of the country of origin.

Printed and bound in Great Britain
by CPI Antony Rowe, Chippenham, Wiltshire

When **Joanna Neil** discovered Mills & Boon®, her lifelong addiction to reading crystallised into an exciting new career writing Mills & Boon® Medical Romance™. Her characters are probably the outcome of her varied lifestyle, which includes working as a clerk, typist, nurse and infant teacher. She enjoys dressmaking and cooking at her Leicestershire home. Her family includes a husband, son and daughter, an exuberant yellow Labrador and two slightly crazed cockatiels. She currently works with a team of tutors at her local education centre, to provide creative writing workshops for people interested in exploring their own writing ambitions.

Recent titles by Joanna Neil:

SHELTERED BY HER TOP-NOTCH BOSS
RETURN OF THE REBEL DOCTOR
HIS BRIDE IN PARADISE
TAMED BY HER BROODING BOSS
DR RIGHT ALL ALONG
DR LANGLEY: PROTECTOR OR PLAYBOY?
A COTSWOLD CHRISTMAS BRIDE
THE TAMING OF DR ALEX DRAYCOTT
BECOMING DR BELLINI'S BRIDE

These books are also available in eBook format from www.millsandboon.co.uk

CHAPTER ONE

So, HERE SHE was at last. Saffi stretched her limbs and walked across the grass to the clifftop railing, where she stood and looked out over the bay. After several hours on the coach, it was good to be out in the fresh air once more.

From here she could see the quay, where fishermen stacked their lobster pots and tended their nets, and for a while she watched the brightly coloured pleasure boats and fishing craft as they tossed gently on the water. Seagulls flew overhead, calling to one another as they soared and dived in search of tasty tidbits.

In the distance, whitewashed cottages nestled amongst the tree-clad hills, where crooked paths twisted and turned on their way down to the harbour. This little corner of Devon looked idyllic. It was so peaceful, so perfect.

If only she could absorb some of that tranquillity. After all, wasn't that why she was here, the reason she had decided to leave everything behind, everything that had represented safety and security in her life—even though in the end that security had turned out to be something of a sham?

A small shiver of panic ran through her. Was she doing the right thing? How could she know what lay ahead? Had she made a big mistake in coming here?

She pulled in a shaky breath, filling her lungs with sea air, and then let it out again slowly, trying to calm herself. She'd been living in Hampshire for the last few years, but this place ought to be familiar to her, or so she'd been told, and it was, in a way, in odd fragments of memory that drifted through her brain, lingered for a moment, and then dissolved in mist as quickly as they'd come.

'Perhaps it's what you need,' her solicitor had said, shuffling the freshly signed papers into a neat bundle and sliding them into a tray on his desk. 'It might do you some good to go back to the place where you spent your childhood. You could at least give it a try.'

'Yes, maybe you're right.'

Now the warm breeze stirred, gently lifting her honey-gold hair and she turned her face towards the sun and felt its caress on her bare arms. Maybe its heat would somehow manage to thaw the chill that had settled around her heart these last few months.

A lone seagull wandered close by, pecking desultorily in the grass, searching for anything edible among the red fescue and the delicate white sea campion. He kept an eye on her, half cautious, half hopeful.

She smiled. 'I'm afraid I don't have any food for you,' she said softly. 'Come to think of it, I haven't actually had anything myself since breakfast.' That seemed an awfully long time ago now, but she'd been thinking so hard about what lay ahead that everything else, even food, had gone from her mind. Not that forgetfulness was unusual for her these days.

'Thanks for reminding me,' she told the bird. 'I should go and find some lunch. Perhaps if you stop by here another day I might have something for you.'

She felt brighter in herself all at once. Coming here had been a big decision for her to make, but it was done. She was here now, and maybe she could look on this as a new beginning.

She moved away from the railing, and glanced around. Her solicitor had made arrangements for her to be met at the Seafarer Inn, which was just across the road from here. It was an attractive-looking building, with lots of polished mahogany timbers decorating the ground-floor frontage and white-painted rendering higher up. There were window-boxes filled with crimson geraniums and trailing surfinias in shades of pink and cream, and in front, on the pavement, there were chalk-boards advertising some of the meals that were on offer.

There was still more than half an hour left before her transport should arrive, plenty of time for her to get some lunch and try to gather her thoughts.

She chose a table by a window, and went over to the bar to place her order. 'I'm expecting a Mr Flynn to meet me here in a while,' she told the landlord, a cheer-ful, friendly man, who was busy polishing glasses with a clean towel. 'Would you mind sending him over to me if he asks?'

'I'll see to it, love. Enjoy your meal.'

'Thanks.'

The solicitor had told her Mr Flynn had been acting as caretaker for the property these last few months. 'He'll give you the keys and show you around. I think he's probably a semi-retired gentleman who's glad to help out. He seems very nice, anyway. When I wrote and told him you don't drive at the moment he offered to come and pick you up.'

So now all she had to do was wait. There was a fluttery feeling in her stomach, but she went back to her table and sat down. She felt conspicuous at first, being here in a bar full of strangers, but now that she was tucked away in the corner she felt much more comfortable, knowing that she was partially shielded by a mahogany lattice.

For her meal, she'd chosen a jacket potato with cheese and a side salad, and she had only just started to eat when a shadow fell across her table. She quickly laid down her fork and looked up to see a man standing there.

Her eyes widened. Was this Mr Flynn? He wasn't at all what she'd been expecting, and her insides made a funny kind of flip-over in response.

Her first impression was that he was in his early thirties, tall, around six feet, and good looking, with strong, angular features and a crop of short, jet-black hair. He was definitely no elderly caretaker, and seeing such a virile young man standing there came as a bit of a shock.

He, in turn, was studying her thoughtfully, a half-smile playing around his mouth, but as his dark grey glance met hers it occurred to her that there was a faintly guarded look about him.

'Saffi?'

'Yes.' She gave him a fleeting smile. 'You must be... You're not quite what I expected...um, you must be Mr Flynn...?'

He frowned, giving her a wary, puzzled glance. 'That's right. Matt Flynn.' There was an odd expression around his eyes and in the slight twist to his mouth as he watched her. He waited a few seconds and then, when she stayed silent, he seemed to brace his shoulders and said in a more businesslike fashion, 'Your solicitor wrote to me. He said you wanted to look over the Moorcroft property.'

'I... Yes, that's right...' She hesitated, suddenly unsure of herself. 'I was hoping I...um...' She glanced unseeingly at the food on her plate. 'I...uh...' She looked up at him once more. 'I didn't mean to keep you waiting. Do you want to leave right away?'

He shook his head. 'No, of course not—not at all. I'm early—go on with your meal, please.' He seemed perplexed, as though he was weighing things up in his mind, but she couldn't imagine what was going on in his head. Something was obviously bothering him.

'Actually,' he said, after a moment or two, 'I'm quite hungry myself. Do you mind if I join you?' He smiled properly then, the corners of his eyes crinkling, his mouth making a crooked shape. 'The food here's very good. The smell of it's tantalising as soon as you walk in the door.'

'Yes, it is.' She began to relax a little and waved him towards a chair. 'Please…have a seat.'

'Okay. I'll just go and order, and be back with you in a minute or two.'

Saffi nodded and watched him as he walked to the bar. His long legs were clad in denim and he was wearing a T-shirt that clung to his chest and emphasised his muscular arms and broad shoulders, causing an unbidden quiver of awareness to clutch at her stomach. Her heart was thudding heavily.

It was strange, acknowledging that she could have such feelings. For so long now it had seemed she'd been going through life on autopilot, stumbling about, trying to cope, and feeling her way through a maze of alien situations. She didn't know where men fitted into all that.

He came back to the table and sat down opposite her, placing a half-pint glass of lager on the table. He studied her thoughtfully. 'Your solicitor said you've been mulling over your options concerning Jasmine Cottage. Are you planning on staying there for a while?' He looked around. 'Only I don't see any luggage, except for a hold-all.'

'No, that's right, I'm having it sent on. I thought it would be easier that way. There's quite a lot of stuff— I'll be staying for a while until I make up my mind what to do…whether to sell up or stay on.'

'Uh-huh.' There was a note of curiosity in his voice as he said, 'I suppose it would have been easier for you if you had a car, but your solicitor said you sold it a few weeks ago?'

'I... Yes. I was... I...' She faltered momentarily. 'It was involved in a rear-end collision and I had it repaired and decided I didn't need a car any more. I lived quite near to the hospital where I worked.'

It was a fair enough excuse, and she didn't want to go into the reasons why she had suddenly lost her confidence behind the wheel. All sorts of daily activities had become a challenge for her in the last few months.

'Ah, I see...at least, I think I do.' He gave her a long, considering look. 'Are you worried about driving for some reason?'

He hadn't believed her lame excuse. She winced. 'Perhaps. A bit. Maybe.' She hoped he wasn't going to ask her any more about it.

He sat back for a moment as the waitress brought his meal, a succulent gammon steak and fries. He was quiet, absorbed in his own thoughts, as though he was troubled by something. Whatever it was, he appeared to cast it aside when the girl had left and said, 'Are you planning on working at a hospital here in Devon?' He sliced into the gammon with his knife.

She shook her head. 'No, at least, not right away. I'm going to take a break for a while.'

It still bothered her that she had to say that, and as she lifted her iced drink to her lips she was dismayed to see that her hand shook a little. She put the glass down and took a deep breath, hoping that he hadn't noticed.

'What about you…what do you do? I'm guessing you're not a semi-retired caretaker, as my solicitor suggested.'

A variety of conflicting emotions crossed his face and Saffi gazed at him uncertainly. He seemed taken aback, somehow, by her question.

His dark brows lifted and his mouth made an ironic twist. After a moment, he said, 'No, actually, caretaking is just a minor part of my week. I'm an A and E doctor, and when I'm not on duty at the hospital I'm on call as a BASICS physician, weekends and evenings mostly.'

Her eyes grew large. 'Oh, I see. We have something in common, then, working in emergency medicine.'

Being a BASICS doctor meant he worked in Immediate Care, as someone who would attend injured people at the roadside, or wherever they happened to be. These doctors usually worked on a voluntary basis, so it was up to the individual doctor if they wanted to take a call.

'Yes, we do.' He nodded, and then looked her over once more, a sober expression on his face. He seemed… resigned almost. 'You don't remember me at all, do you?'

Saffi's jaw dropped in consternation. 'Remember you? Should I?' No wonder his manner had seemed so strange. Her stomach was leaden. So much for a new beginning. Even here it seemed she had come face to face with her vulnerabilities. 'Have we met before?'

'Oh, yes. We have.' He said it in a confident, firm voice and she floundered for a second or two, thrown on to the back foot. Of course there would be people here she had known in the past.

'I'm sorry.' She sent him a worried glance. 'Perhaps it

was some time ago?' She was desperately hoping that his answer would smooth away any awful gaffe on her part.

'We worked together at a hospital in London.'

'Oh.' Anxiety washed over her. 'Perhaps you were working in a different specialty to me?'

He nodded. 'That's true, I was working in the trauma unit. But I definitely remember you. How could I forget?' His glance moved over her face, taking in the soft blush of her cheeks and the shining hair that fell in a mass of soft curls around her face. His eyes darkened as though he was working through some unresolved torment.

She exhaled slowly, only then realising that she'd been holding her breath. 'What were the chances that we would run into each other again here in Devon?' she said, trying to make light of things, but she looked at him with troubled blue eyes.

'I guess it was bound to happen some time. After all, we both knew your aunt, didn't we? That's another thing we have in common, isn't it?'

She hesitated. 'Is it? I…I don't know,' she said at last on a brief sigh. He'd taken the trouble to come here, and said they knew one another—perhaps she owed him some kind of explanation.

'The thing is, Matt, something happened to me a few months ago…there was an accident, and I ended up with a head injury. I don't remember exactly what went on, only that I woke up in hospital and everything that had gone before was a blank.'

He made a sharp intake of breath. 'I'm sorry.' He shook his head as though he was trying to come to terms with what she had told him. 'Your solicitor mentioned you had some problems with your memory, but I'd no idea it was so profound.' He reached for her, cupping his hand over hers. 'What kind of accident was it? Don't you remember anything at all?'

'Not much.' His hand was warm and comforting, enveloping hers. He was a complete stranger to her, and yet she took heart from that instinctive, compassionate action.

'They told me I must have fallen down the stairs and banged my head. I shared a house with another girl—my flat was on the upper floor—and apparently my friend found me when she came home at the end of her shift at the hospital. She called for an ambulance, and they whisked me away to Accident and Emergency.'

She went over the events in her mind. 'It turned out I had a fractured skull. The emergency team looked after me, and after that it was just a question of waiting for the brain swelling to go down, so that they could assess the amount of neurological damage I had been left with. I was lucky, in a way, because there's been no lasting physical harm—nothing that you can see.' She gave a brief smile. 'Except for my hair, of course. It used to be long and shoulder length, but they had to shave part of my head.'

'Your hair looks lovely. It suits you like that.'

'Thank you.' She moved restlessly, and he released her so that she was free to take another sip of her cold drink. Her throat was dry, aching. 'I remember bits and pieces. Some things come back to me every now and again, and I manage to keep hold of them. Other memories seem to float around for a while and then disappear before I can picture them clearly.'

'I'm so sorry, Saffi. I can't imagine what that must be like.' His grey eyes were sombre and sympathetic. 'You must be taking a leap in the dark, coming here, away from everything you've known for the last few years. Or perhaps you remember Devon, and Jasmine Cottage?'

She frowned. 'No. I don't think so. Some of it, perhaps.' Her lips flattened briefly. 'I'm hoping it'll all come back to me when I get to the house.'

He nodded. 'I was really sorry when your aunt died. She was a lovely woman.'

'Yes.' She said it cautiously, unwilling to admit that she couldn't remember very much about the woman who had left her this property in a picturesque village situated near the Devon coast. Everyone told her they'd been very close, but the sad truth was she simply had no clear recollection of her benefactor. It seemed wrong to come here to take up an inheritance in those awful circumstances, but all those who knew her back in Hampshire had persuaded her it was the right thing to do. Only time would tell.

'Apparently she died before I had my accident, and I'd been to her funeral. All this business with the property had to be put to one side while I was recovering in hospital.' She glanced at him. 'Had you known my aunt for a long time?' She was suddenly keen to know how he was connected to her relative, and how he came to be caretaking the property.

He appeared to hesitate before answering and she wondered if this was something she ought to have known, some part of the way they'd known one another. 'We met a few years back, but then I went to work with the air ambulance in Wales, so I didn't see much of her until I came to work in Devon last summer. After that, she called on me from time to time to help fix things about the place.'

'I'm glad she had someone. Thanks for that.' She smiled at him, and made light conversation with him while they finished their meals. Her emotions were in a precarious state and she didn't want to enquire right then into how she'd known Matt in the past. Perhaps he understood that, or maybe he had his own reasons for not bringing it up. He seemed concerned, and clearly he had been thrown off balance by her loss of memory.

They left the inn together a short time later and went to his car, a fairly new rapid-response vehicle equipped with a blue light, high-visibility strips and badges.

He held open the passenger door for her and she slipped into the seat. The smell of luxurious soft leather greeted her, and she sat back and tried to relax.

Matt set the car in motion and started along the coast road, cruising at a moderate pace so she had the chance to take in the scenery on the way.

She gazed out of the window, watching the harbour slowly recede, and in a while they left the blue sweep of the bay behind them as he drove inland towards the hills. The landscape changed to rolling green vistas interspersed with narrow lanes lined with clusters of pretty cottages decorated with hanging baskets full of bright flowers.

He sent her a quick, sideways glance. 'Is this meant to be a kind of holiday for you—a chance to recover from everything that has happened? Or are you more concerned with sorting out your aunt's estate?'

'I suppose it's a bit of both, really. I was beginning to feel that I needed a break, a change of scenery at least, and although it was a sad thing that my aunt passed on, it gave me an opportunity to get away. I...' She hesitated momentarily, then went on, 'There's no one else left in my family, so it's down to me to sort out what's to be done with the property.'

Perhaps she'd managed to come to terms with all that before the accident, but since then she'd felt her isolation keenly. Being unable to remember people around her meant that she was cut off from all that was familiar, and it left her with an acute sense of loneliness.

'And do you think you'll manage all right?' he said, cutting in on her thoughts. 'If you're not working, I mean?' He saw her hesitation and pulled a wry face. 'Am I overstepping the mark? You'll have to let me know if I do that—I'm afraid I tend to get carried away and say what's on my mind. '

She shook her head. 'That's all right. I appreciate you being open with me.' She frowned. 'I'm not sure how I'd handle going back to medicine just yet. But I have enough money to keep me going for now, until I find my feet. After my parents died some years ago, it seems that

I sold the property and invested what they left me. So at least I don't have any worries on that score.'

'Perhaps that's just as well. It looks as though you have more than enough on your plate right now.'

He concentrated on the road for a while as he negotiated a series of bends, and then, after following a winding country lane for about half a mile, Saffi suddenly became aware of an isolated farmhouse coming into view. It was set back from the road amidst fields, a little gem in the surrounding greenery.

'That's the house, isn't it?' she said, excitement growing inside her as they drew closer. It was a long, rambling property, with a couple of side-on extensions that had been added to the main house over the years, giving it three different roof elevations. It was pleasing on the eye, with the traditional white rendering throughout and slate roofs over all. The window-frames were mahogany, as was the front door. A trailing jasmine shrub sprawled over the entrance wall, its bright, yellow flowers making a beautiful contrast to the dark evergreen leaves.

'Do you remember it?'

'No. But my solicitor showed me a photograph. It's lovely, isn't it?'

He nodded, and parked the car on the drive. 'Here, you'll need the keys.'

'Thank you.' She stood for a moment or two, gazing at the house, and then she slowly walked up to the front door. The scent of jasmine filled the air, sweetly sensuous, instantly calming. Saffi breathed it in and suddenly she was overwhelmed as her mind captured the image of a dear, slender woman, a nurturing, gentle soul.

'Oh…Annie…Annie…'

Her eyes filled with tears, the breath caught in her throat, and she heard Matt saying urgently, 'What is it, Saffi? What's wrong? Have you remembered something?'

She was shaking. 'My aunt…it was just as though she was here…I could feel her… But she's gone, and I don't think I can bear it…'

He hesitated momentarily, and then wrapped his arms around her. 'It's all right, Saffi. I know it's hard, but it's good that you remember her.'

She didn't move for several minutes, overtaken by grief, but secure in his embrace, glad of the fact that he was holding her, because but for that she might have fallen. Her legs were giving way as emotion wreaked havoc with her body, leaving her fragile, helpless.

'I'm sorry,' she said after a while, ashamed of her weakness and brushing away her tears with her fingers. 'The memory of her just came flooding back. I wasn't expecting it.'

'Do you remember anything else?' he asked cautiously. 'About the house, your work…your friends?' He was looking at her intently, and perhaps he was asking if she had begun to remember anything at all about him and the way they'd known one another.

She shook her head. 'All I know is that I was happy here. I felt safe. This is home.'

He let out a long breath, and then straightened up, as

though in that moment he'd come to some sort of decision. 'Well, that's good. That's a start.' He didn't add anything more, didn't try to tell her about the past, or give any hint as to what their relationship might have been. Instead, he seemed to make an effort to pull himself together, reluctantly releasing her when she felt ready to turn back towards the door.

'I should go in,' she said.

'Do you want me to go in with you? You might still be a bit shaky…and perhaps I ought to show you around and explain what needs to be done with the animals. I mean, I can look after them till you find your feet, but maybe you'll want to take over at some point.'

She stared at him. 'Animals?'

'You don't know about them?'

She shook her head. 'It's news to me.' She frowned. 'You're right. Perhaps you'd better come in and explain things to me.'

They went into the house, and Saffi walked slowly along the hallway, waiting in vain for more memories to come back to her. Matt showed her into the kitchen and she looked around, pleased with the homely yet modern look of the room. The units were cream coloured and there were open shelves and glass-fronted cabinets on the walls. A smart black cooker was fitted into the newly painted fireplace recess, and an oak table stood in the centre of the room.

'I bought some food for you and stocked the refrigerator when I heard you were coming over here,' Matt said. 'Your solicitor said you might need time to settle in before you started to get organised.'

She smiled. 'Thanks. That was thoughtful of you.' She checked the fridge and some of the cupboards and chuckled. 'This is better stocked than my kitchen back in Hampshire. We were always running out of stuff over there these last few months. I had to write notes to remind myself to shop, because my flatmate was worse than me at organisation.'

'I can see I'll need to keep an eye on you,' he murmured. 'We can't have you wasting away.' His glance ran over her and a flush of heat swept along her cheekbones. She was wearing jeans that moulded themselves to her hips and a camisole top that outlined her feminine curves, and she suddenly felt self-conscious under that scorching gaze.

'I...uh...I'll show you the rest of the house if you like,' he said, walking towards a door at the side of the room. 'Unless it's all coming back to you?'

She shook her head. 'It isn't, I'm afraid.' She followed him into the dining room, where the furniture followed the design of the kitchen. There was a cream wood Welsh dresser displaying patterned plates, cups and saucers, and a matching table and upholstered chairs.

'The sitting room's through here,' Matt said, leading the way into a sunlit room where wide patio doors led on to a paved terrace.

She glanced around. It was a lovely room, with accents of warm colour and a sofa that looked soft and comfortable.

'I think you'll find it's cosy of an evening with the log-burning stove,' he murmured.

'Yes.' She had a fleeting image of a woman adding logs to the stove, and a lump formed in her throat.

'Are you okay?'

She nodded. 'I guess I'll need a plentiful supply of wood, then,' she said, getting a grip on herself. 'Where did my aunt get her logs from, do you know?'

'There's a copse on the land—your land. It should supply plenty of fuel for some time to come, but your aunt did a lot of replanting. Anyway, I've filled up the log store for you, so you won't need to worry about that for quite a while.'

'It sounds as though I owe you an awful lot,' she said with a frown. 'What with the groceries, the wood and...you mentioned there were animals. I don't think I've ever had any experience looking after pets—none that I recall, anyway.' Yet no dog or cat had come running to greet them when they'd first entered the house. It was very puzzling.

'Ah...yes. We'll do a quick tour upstairs and then I'll take you to see them.'

There were two bedrooms upstairs, one with an en suite bathroom, and along the corridor was the main bathroom. Saffi couldn't quite work out the layout up here. There were fewer rooms than she'd expected, as though something was missing, but perhaps her senses were off somehow.

'Okay, shall we go and solve the mystery of these pets?' she murmured. Maybe her aunt had a small aviary outside. She'd heard quite a bit of birdsong when they'd arrived, but there were a good many trees around the house that would have accounted for that.

They went outside to the garden, and Saffi caught her breath as she looked out at the extent of her property. It wasn't just a garden, there was also a paddock and a stable block nearby.

'Oh, no. Tell me it's not horses,' she pleaded. 'I don't know anything about looking after them.'

'Just a couple.' He saw her look of dismay and relented. 'No, actually, Annie mainly used the stable block as a store for the fruit harvest.'

She breathed a small sigh of relief.

Fruit harvest, he'd said. Saffi made a mental note of that. On the south side of the garden she'd noticed an archway in a stone wall, and something flickered in her faulty memory banks. Could it be a walled garden? From somewhere in the depths of her mind she recalled images of fruit trees and glasshouses with grapes, melons and peaches.

They walked by the stable block and came to a fenced-off area that contained a hen hut complete with a large covered wire run. Half a dozen hens wandered about in there , pecking the ground for morsels of food.

'Oh, my...' Saffi's eyes widened. 'Was there anything else my aunt was into? Anything I should know about? I mean, should I ever want to go back to medicine, I don't know how I'll find the time to fit it in, what with fruit picking, egg gathering and keeping track of this huge garden.'

He laughed. 'She was quite keen on beekeeping. There are three hives in the walled garden.'

Saffi rolled her eyes. 'Maybe I should turn around right now and head back for Hampshire.'

'I don't think so. I hope you won't do that.' He gave her a long look. 'I don't see you as a quitter. Anyway, it's not that difficult. I'll show you. Let's go and make a start with the hens.'

He led the way to the coop. 'I let them out in the morning,' he explained. 'They have food pellets in feeders, as well as water, but in the afternoon or early evening, whenever I finish work, I give them a mix of corn and split peas. There's some oyster shell and grit mixed in with it, so it's really good for them.' He went over to a wooden store shed and brought out a bucket filled with corn. 'Do you want to sprinkle some on the ground for them?'

'Uh…okay.' This had all come as a bit of a jolt to her. Instead of the peace and quiet she'd been expecting, the chance to relax and get herself back together again after the trauma of the last few months, it was beginning to look as though her days would be filled with stuff she'd never done before.

She went into the covered run, leaving Matt to shut the door and prevent any attempted escapes. An immediate silence fell as the birds took in her presence.

'Here you go,' she said, scattering the corn around her, and within seconds she found herself surrounded by hens. Some even clambered over her feet to get to the grain. Gingerly, she took a step forward, but they ignored her and simply went on eating. She shot Matt a quick look of consternation and he grinned.

'Problem?' he asked, and she pulled a face.

'What do I do now?'

He walked towards her and grasped her hand. 'You just have to force your way through. Remember, you're the one in charge here, not the hens.'

'Hmm, if you say so.'

He was smiling as he pulled her out of the run and shut the door behind them. 'They need to be back into the coop by nightfall. As long as their routine isn't disturbed, things should go smoothly enough. They're laying very well at the moment, so you'll have a good supply of eggs.'

'Oh, well, that's a plus, I suppose.'

He sent her an amused glance. 'That's good. At least you're beginning to look on the positive side.'

She gritted her teeth but stayed silent. Now he was patronising her. Her head was starting to ache, a throbbing beat pounding at her temples.

'And the beehives?' she asked. 'What's to be done with them?'

'Not much, at this time of year. You just keep an eye on them to make sure everything's all right and let them get on with making honey. Harvesting is done round about the end of August, beginning of September.'

'You make it sound so easy. I guess I'll have to find myself a book on beekeeping.'

'I think Annie had several of those around the place.'

They made their way back to the house, and Saffi said

quietly, 'I should thank you for everything you've done here since my aunt died. I'd no idea the caretaking was so involved. You've managed to keep this place going, and I'm very grateful to you for that.'

'Well, I suppose I had a vested interest.'

She frowned. 'You did?'

He nodded. 'Your aunt made me a beneficiary of her will. Didn't your solicitor tell you about it?'

She stared at him. 'No. At least, I don't think so.' She searched her mind for details of her conversations with the solicitor. There had been several over the last few weeks, and maybe he'd mentioned something about another beneficiary. She'd assumed he meant there was a small bequest to a friend or neighbour.

The throbbing in her temple was clouding her thinking. 'He said he didn't want to bother me with all the details because of my problems since the accident.'

He looked at her quizzically and she added briefly, 'Headaches and so on. I had a short attention span for a while, and I can be a bit forgetful at times…but I'm much better now. I feel as though I'm on the mend.'

'I'm sure you are. You seem fairly clear-headed to me.'

'I'm glad you think so.' She studied him. 'So, what exactly did you inherit…a sum of money, a share in the proceeds from the livestock…the tools in the garden store?' She said it in a light-hearted manner, but it puzzled her as to what her aunt could have left him.

'Uh…it was a bit more than that, actually.' He looked a trifle uneasy, and perhaps that was because he'd assumed she'd known all about it in advance. But then he seemed to throw off any doubts he might have had and said briskly, 'Come on, I'll show you.'

He went to the end extension of the property and unlocked a separate front door, standing back and waving her inside.

Saffi stared about her in a daze. 'But this is… I didn't notice this before…' She was completely taken aback by this new discovery. She was standing in a beautifully furnished living room, and through an archway she glimpsed what looked like a kitchen-diner, fitted out with golden oak units.

'Originally, the house was one large, complete family home, but your aunt had some alterations made,' he said. 'There's a connecting door to your part of the house and another upstairs. They're locked, so we'll be completely separate—you'll have a key amongst those I gave you.'

She looked at the connecting door, set unobtrusively into an alcove in the living room.

'I'll show you the rest of the house,' he said, indicating an open staircase in the corner of the room.

She followed him up the stairs, her mind reeling under this new, stunning revelation. No wonder she'd thought there was something missing from the upper floor when he'd taken her to look around. The missing portion was right here, in the form of a good-sized bedroom and bathroom.

'You're very quiet,' he murmured.

'I'm trying to work out how this came about,' she said

in a soft voice. 'You're telling me that my aunt left this part of the house to you?'

'She did. I'd no idea that she had written it into her will or that she planned to do it. She didn't mention it to me. Does it bother you?'

'I think it does, yes.'

It wasn't that she wanted it for herself. Heaven forbid, she hadn't even remembered this house existed until her solicitor had brought it to her attention. But her aunt couldn't have known this man very long—by his own account he'd only been in the area for a few months. And yet she'd left him a sizeable property. How had that come about?

All at once she needed to be on her own so that she could think things through. 'I should go,' she said. 'I think I need time to take this in. But…thanks for showing me around.'

'You're welcome.' He went with her down the stairs. 'Any time you need me, Saffi, I'll be here.'

She nodded. That was certainly true. His presence gave a new meaning to the words 'next-door neighbour'.

She'd come here expecting to find herself in a rural hideout, well away from anyone and anything, so that she might finally recuperate from the devastating head injury that had left her without any knowledge of family or friends. And none of it was turning out as she'd hoped.

Matt had seemed such a charming, likeable man, but wasn't that the way of all confidence tricksters? How could she know what to think?

Her instincts had been all over the place since the accident, and perhaps she was letting that trauma sour her judgement. Ever since she'd woken up in hospital she'd had the niggling suspicion that all was not as it seemed as far as her fall was concerned.

She'd done what she could to put that behind her, but now the question was, could she put her trust in Matt, who seemed so obliging? What could have convinced her aunt to leave him such a substantial inheritance?

CHAPTER TWO

SAFFI FINISHED WEEDING the last of the flower borders in the walled garden and leaned back on her heels to survey her handiwork. It was a beautiful garden, filled with colour and sweet scents, just perfect for the bees that flew from flower to flower, gathering nectar and pollen. Against the wall, the pale pink of the hollyhocks was a lovely contrast to the deep rose colour of the flamboyant peonies. Close by, tall delphiniums matched the deep blue of the sky.

'You've been keeping busy, from the looks of things,' Matt commented, startling her as he appeared in the archway that separated this part of the garden from the larger, more general area. 'You've done a good job here.'

She lifted her head to look at him, causing her loosely pinned curls to quiver with the movement. He started to walk towards her, and straight away her pulse went into overdrive and her heart skipped a beat. He was overwhelmingly masculine, with a perfect physique, his long legs encased in blue jeans while his muscular chest and arms were emphasised by the dark T-shirt he was wearing.

'Thanks.' She viewed him cautiously. She hadn't seen much of him this last week, and perhaps that was just as well, given her concerns about him. In fact, she'd wondered if he'd deliberately stayed away from her, giving her room to sort herself out. Though, of course, he must have been out at work for a good deal of the time.

It was hard to know what to think of him. He'd said they'd known one another before this, and she wanted to trust him, but the circumstances of his inheritance had left her thoroughly confused and made her want to tread carefully where he was concerned. What could have led her aunt to leave the house to be shared by two people? It was very odd.

To give Matt his due, though, he'd kept this place going after Aunt Annie's death—he'd had the leaky barn roof fixed, her closest neighbours told her, and he'd made sure the lawns were trimmed regularly. He'd taken good care of the hens, too, and she ought to be grateful to him for all that.

'I see you've made a start on picking the fruit.' He looked at the peach tree, trained in a fan shape across the south wall where it received the most sunshine. Nearby there were raspberry canes, alongside blackberry and redcurrant bushes.

She gave a wry smile. 'Yes…I only had to touch the peaches and they came away from the branches, so I guessed it was time to gather them in. And I had to pick the raspberries before the birds made away with the entire crop. Actually, I've put some of the fruit to one side for you, back in the kitchen. I was going to bring it over to you later today.'

'That was good of you. Thanks.' He smiled, looking at her appreciatively, his glance wandering slowly over her slender yet curvaceous figure, and making the breath catch in her throat. She was wearing light blue denim shorts and a crop top with thin straps that left her arms bare and revealed the pale gold of her midriff. All at once, under that all-seeing gaze, she felt decidedly un-derdressed. Her face flushed with heat, probably from a combination of the burning rays of the sun and the fact that he was standing beside her, making her conscious of her every move.

She took off her gardening gloves and brushed a stray tendril of honey-blonde hair from her face with the back of her hand. 'There's so much produce, I'm not quite sure what my aunt did with it all. I thought I might take some along to the neighbours along the lane.'

'I'm sure they'll appreciate that. Annie sold some of it, flowers, too, and eggs, to the local shopkeepers, and there were always bunches of cut flowers on sale by the roadside at the front of the house, along with baskets of fruit. She trusted people to put the money in a box, and apparently they never let her down.'

'That sounds like a good idea. I'll have to try it,' she said, getting to her feet. She was a bit stiff from being in the same position for so long, and he put out a hand to help her up.

'Thanks.' His grasp was strong and supportive and that unexpected human contact was strangely comfort-

ing. Warm colour brushed her cheeks once more as his
gaze travelled fleetingly over her long, shapely legs.

'You could do with a gardener's knee pad—one of
those covered foam things…'

'Yes, you're probably right.' She frowned. 'I'm beginning to think that looking after this property and the
land and everything that comes with it is going to be a
full-time job.'

'It is, especially at this time of year,' he agreed. 'But
maybe you could get someone in to help out if it becomes
too much for you to handle. Funds permitting, of course.'

She nodded, going over to one of the redwood garden
chairs and sitting down. 'I suppose, sooner or later, I'll
have to make up my mind what I'm going to do.'

She waved him to the seat close by. A small table connected the two chairs, and on it she had laid out a glass
jug filled with iced apple juice. She lifted the cover that
was draped over it to protect the contents from the sunshine. 'Would you like a cold drink?'

'That'd be great, thanks.' He came to sit beside her
and she brought out a second glass from the cupboard
beneath the table.

She filled both glasses, passing one to him before
she drank thirstily from hers. 'It's lovely out here, so se-
rene, but it's really hot today. Great if you're relaxing but
not so good when you're working.' She lifted the glass,
pressing it against her forehead to savour the coolness.

'How are you coping, generally?'

'All right, I think. I came here to rest and recuperate
but the way things turned out it's been good for me to

keep busy. I've been exploring the village and the sea-
side in between looking after this place. The only thing
I've left completely alone is anything to do with the beehives. I think I'm supposed to have equipment of some
sort, aren't I, before I go near them?'

'There are a couple of outfits in the stable block. I
can show you how to go on with them, whenever you're
ready.'

She nodded. 'Thanks. I'll take you up on that. I'm
just not quite ready to tackle beekeeping on my own.'
She drank more juice and studied him musingly. Despite
her reservations about him, this was one area where
she'd better let him guide her. 'Did you help my aunt
with the hives?'

'I did, from time to time. She needed some repairs
done to the stands and while I was doing that she told
me all about looking after them. She said she talked to
the bees, told them what was happening in her life—I
don't think she was serious about that, but she seemed
to find it calming and it helped to clear her thoughts.'

'Hmm. Perhaps I should try it. Maybe it will help me
get my mind back together.'

'How's that going?'

She pulled a face. 'I recall bits and pieces every now
and again. Especially when I'm in the house or out here,
in the garden...not so much in the village and round
about. I was told Aunt Annie brought me up after my
parents died, and I know...I feel inside...that she loved
me as if I was her own daughter.'

Her voice faltered. 'I...I miss her. I keep seeing her

as a lively, wonderful old lady, but she was frail towards the end, wasn't she? That's what the solicitor said…that she had a heart attack, but I don't remember any of that.'

'Perhaps your mind is blocking it out.'

'Yes, that might be it. Even so, I feel as though I'm grieving inside, even though I can't remember everything.' She was troubled. Wouldn't Matt have been here when she had come back to see her aunt, and again at the time of the funeral? Everyone told her she'd done that, that she'd visited regularly, yet she had no memory of it, or of him.

She straightened her shoulders, glancing at him. 'Anyway, I'm glad I came back to this house. I was in two minds about it at first, but somehow I feel at peace here, as though this is where I belong.'

'I'm glad about that. Annie would have been pleased.'

'Yes, I think she would.' She studied him thoughtfully. 'It sounds as though you knew her well—even though you had only been back here for a short time.'

She hesitated for a moment and then decided to say what was on her mind. 'How was it that you came to be living here?' She wasn't sure what she expected him to say. He would hardly admit to wheedling his way into an elderly lady's confidence, would he?

He lifted his glass and took a long swallow of the cold liquid. Saffi watched him, mesmerised by the movement of his sun-bronzed throat, and by the way his strong fingers gripped the glass.

He placed it back on the table a moment later. 'I'd started a new job in the area and I was looking for a place to live. Accommodation was in short supply, it being the height of the holiday season, but I managed to find a flat near the hospital. It was a bit basic, though, and after a while I began to hanker for a few home comforts...'

'Oh? Such as...?' She raised a quizzical brow and he grinned.

'Hot and cold running water, for a start, and some means of preparing food. There was a gas ring, but it took forever to heat a pan of beans. And as to the plumbing—I was lucky if it worked at all. It was okay taking cold baths in the summer, but come wintertime it was bracing, to say the least. I spoke to the landlord about it, but he kept making excuses and delaying—he obviously didn't want to spend money on getting things fixed.'

'So my aunt invited you stay here?'

He nodded. 'I'd been helping her out by doing repairs about the place, and one day she suggested that I move into the annexe.'

'That must have been a relief to you.'

He smiled. 'Yes, it was. Best of all was the home-cooked food—I wasn't expecting that, but she used to bring me pot roasts or invite me round to her part of the house for dinner of an evening. I think she liked to have company.'

'Yes, that was probably it.' Her mouth softened at the image of her aunt befriending this young doctor. 'I suppose the hot and cold running water goes without saying?'

'That, too.'

She sighed. 'I wish I could say the same about mine.

I would have loved to take a shower after doing all that weeding, but something seems to have gone wrong with it. I tried to get hold of a plumber, but apparently they're all too busy to come out and look at it. Three weeks is the earliest date I could get.'

He frowned. 'Have you any idea why it stopped working? Perhaps it's something simple, like the shower head being blocked with calcium deposits?'

'It isn't that. I checked. I've a horrible feeling it's to do with the electronics—I suppose in the end I'll have to buy a new shower.' Her mouth turned down a fraction.

'Would you like me to have a look at it? You never know, between the two of us, we might be able to sort it out, or at least find out what's gone wrong.'

'Are you sure you wouldn't mind doing that?' She felt a small ripple of relief flow through her. He might not know much at all about plumbing, but just to have a second opinion would be good.

'I'd be glad to. Shall we go over to the house now, if you've finished what you were doing out here?'

'Okay.' They left the walled garden, passing through the stone archway, and then followed the path to the main house. Out in the open air, the hens clucked and foraged in the run amongst the patches of grass and gravel for grain and food pellets, and ignored them completely.

'So, what happened when you tried to use the shower last time?' Matt asked as they went upstairs a few minutes later.

'I switched on the isolator switch as usual outside the bathroom and everything was fine. But after I'd switched off the shower I noticed that the isolator switch was stuck in the on position. The light comes on, but the water isn't coming through.'

'I'll start with the switch, then. Do you have a screwdriver? Otherwise I'll go and get one from my place.'

'The toolbox is downstairs. I'll get it for you.'

'Thanks. I'll turn off the miniature circuit-breaker.'

He went off to disconnect the electricity and a few minutes later he unscrewed the switch and began to inspect it. 'It looks as though this is the problem,' he said, showing her. 'The connections are blackened.'

'Is that bad? Do I need to be worried about the wiring?'

He shook his head. 'It often happens with these things. They burn out. I'll pick up another switch from the supplier in town and get someone to come over and fix it for you. I know an electrician who works at the hospital—I'll ask him to call in.'

'Oh, that's brilliant...' She frowned. 'If he'll do it, that is...'

'He will. He owes me a favour or two, so I'm sure he won't mind turning out for this. In the meantime, if you want to get a few things together—you can come over to my place to use the shower, if you like?'

'Really?' Her eyes widened and she gave him a grateful smile. 'I'd like that very much, thank you.'

She hurried away to collect a change of clothes and a towel, everything that she thought she would need, and then they went over to his part of the house.

She looked around. The first time she had been here

she'd been so taken aback by his revelation about the inheritance, and everything had been a bit of a blur, so she hadn't taken much in.

But now she saw that his living room was large and airy, with a wide window looking out on to a well-kept lawn and curved flower borders. He'd kept the furnishing in here simple, uncluttered, with two cream-coloured sofas and an oak coffee table that had pleasing granite tile inserts. There was a large, flat-screen TV on the wall. The floor was golden oak, partially covered by an oriental patterned rug. It was a beautiful, large annexe—what could have persuaded Aunt Annie to leave him all this?

'I'm afraid I'm on call today with the first-response team,' he said, cutting into her thoughts, 'so if I have to leave while you're in the shower, just help yourself to whatever you need—there's tea and coffee in the kitchen and cookies in the jar. Otherwise I'll be waiting for you in here.'

He paused, sending her a look that was part teasing, part hopeful. Heat glimmered in the depths of his grey eyes. 'Unless, of course, you need a hand with anything in the bathroom? I'd be happy to help out. More than happy…'

She gave a soft, uncertain laugh, not quite sure how to respond to that. 'Well, uh…that's a great offer, but I think I'll manage, thanks.'

He contrived to look disappointed and amused all at the same time. 'Ah, well…another day, perhaps?'

'In your dreams,' she murmured.

She went upstairs to the bathroom, still thinking about his roguish suggestion. It was hard to admit, but she was actually more than tempted. He was strong, incredibly good looking, hugely charismatic and very capable...he'd shown that he was very willing to help out with anything around the place.

So why had she turned him down? She was a free spirit after all, with no ties. The truth was, she'd no idea how she'd been before, but right now she was deeply wary of rushing into anything, and she'd only known him for a very short time.

Or had she? He'd said they'd known one another for quite a while, years, in fact. What kind of relationship had that been? For his part, he was definitely interested in her and he certainly seemed keen to take things further.

But she still wasn't sure she could trust him. He was charming, helpful, competent...weren't those the very qualities that might have made her aunt want to bequeath him part of her home?

She sighed. It was frustrating to have so many unanswered questions.

Going into the bathroom, she tried to push those thoughts to one side as she looked around. This room was all pearly white, with gleaming, large rectangular tiles on the wall, relieved by deeply embossed border tiles in attractive pastel colours. There was a bath, along with the usual facilities, and in the corner there was a beautiful, curved, glass-fronted shower cubicle.

Under the shower spray, she tried to relax and let the

warm water soothe away her troubled thoughts. Perhaps she should learn to trust, and take comfort in the knowledge that Matt had only ever been kind to her.

So far, he had been there for her, doing his best to help her settle in. She had been the only stumbling block to his initial efforts by being suspicious of his motives around her aunt. Perhaps she should do her best to be a little more open to him.

Afterwards, she towelled her hair dry and put on fresh clothes, jeans that clung to her in all the right places, and a short-sleeved T-shirt the same blue as her eyes. She didn't want to go downstairs with wet hair, but there was no hairdryer around so she didn't really have a choice. Still, even when damp her hair curled riotously, so perhaps she didn't look too bad.

Anyway, if Matt had been called away to work, it wouldn't matter how she looked, would it?

'Hi.' He smiled as she walked into the living room. 'You look fresh and wholesome—like a beautiful water nymph.'

She returned his smile. 'Thanks. And thanks for letting me use the shower. Perhaps I ought to go back to my place and find my hairdryer.'

'Do you have to do that? I'm making some lunch for us. I heard the shower switch off, so I thought you might soon be ready to eat. We could take the food outside, if you want. The sun will dry your hair.'

'Oh…okay. I wasn't expecting that. It sounds good.'

They went outside on to a small, paved terrace, and he set out food on a wrought-iron table, inviting her to sit down while he went to fetch cold drinks. He'd made pizza slices, topped with mozzarella cheese, tomato and peppers, along with a crisp side salad.

He came back holding a tray laden with glass tumblers and a jug of mixed red fruit juice topped with slices of apple, lemon and orange.

'I can bring you some wine, if you prefer,' he said, sitting down opposite her. 'I can't have any myself in case I have to go out on a job.'

'No, this will be fine,' she told him. 'It looks wonderful.'

'It is. Wait till you taste it.'

The food was good, and the juice, which had a hint of sparkling soda water in it, was even better than it looked. 'This has been a real treat for me,' she said a little later, when they'd finished a simple dessert of ice cream and fresh raspberries. 'Everything was delicious.' She mused on that for a moment. 'I don't remember when someone last prepared a meal for me.'

'I'm glad you enjoyed it.' He sent her a sideways glance. 'Actually, Annie made meals for both of us sometimes—whenever you came over here to visit she would cook, or put out buffet-style food, or occasionally she would ask me to organise the barbecue so that we could eat outside and enjoy the summer evenings. Sometimes she would ask the neighbours to join us.' He watched her carefully. 'Don't you have any memory of that?'

'No...' She tried to think about it, grasping at fleeting images with her mind, but in the end she had to admit defeat. Then a stray vision came out of nowhere, and she said quickly, 'Except—there was one time… I think I'd been out somewhere—to work, or to see friends—then somehow I was back here and everything was wrong.'

He straightened up, suddenly taut and a bit on edge. Distracted, she sent him a bewildered glance. 'I don't know what happened, but the feelings are all mixed up inside me. I know I was desperately unhappy and I think Aunt Annie put her arms around me to comfort me.' She frowned. 'How can I not remember? It's as though I'm distracted all the while, all over the place in my head. Why am I like this?'

It was a plea for help and he said softly, 'You probably feel that way because it's as though part of you is missing. Your mind is still the one bit of you that needs to heal. And perhaps deep down, for some reason, you're rejecting what's already there, hidden inside you. Give it time. Don't try so hard, and I expect it'll come back to you in a few weeks or months.'

'Weeks or months…when am I ever going to get back to normal?' There was a faint thread of despair in her voice. 'I should be working, earning a living, but how do I do that when I don't even know what it's like to be a doctor?'

He didn't answer. His phone rang at that moment, cutting through their conversation, and she noticed that the call came on a different mobile from his everyday phone. He immediately became alert.

'It's a job,' he said, when he had finished speaking to Ambulance Control, 'so I have to go. I'm sorry to leave you, Saffi, but I'm the nearest responder.'

'Do you know what it is, what's happened?'

He nodded. 'A six-year-old boy has been knocked down by a car. The paramedics are asking for a doctor to attend.' He stood up, grim-faced, and made to walk across the terrace, but then he stopped and looked back at her. He made as if to say something and then stopped.

'What is it?' she asked.

He shook his head. 'It's nothing.'

He made to turn away again and she said quickly, 'Tell me what's on your mind, please.'

'I wondered if you might want to come with me? It might be good for you to be out there again, to get a glimpse of the working world. Then again, this might not be the best call out for you, at this time.' He frowned. 'It could be bad.'

She hesitated, overwhelmed by a moment of panic, a feeling of dread that ripped through her, but he must have read her thoughts because he said in a calm voice, 'You wouldn't have to do anything. Just observe.'

She sucked in a deep breath. 'All right. I'll do it.' It couldn't be so bad if she wasn't called on to make any decisions, could it? But this was a young child…that alone was enough to make her balk at the prospect. Should she change her mind?

Matt was already heading out to the garage, and she hurried after him. This was no time to be dithering.

They slid into the seats of the rapid-response vehicle, a car that came fully equipped for emergency medical situations, and within seconds Matt had set the sat nav and was driving at speed towards the scene of the accident. He switched on the flashing blue light and the siren and Saffi tried to keep a grip on herself. All she had to do was observe, he'd said. Nothing more. She repeated it to herself over and over, as if by doing that she would manage to stay calm.

'This is the place.'

Saffi took in everything with a glance. A couple of policemen were here, questioning bystanders and organising traffic diversions. An ambulance stood by, its rear doors open, and a couple of paramedics hid her view of the injured child. A woman was there, looking distraught. Saffi guessed she was the boy's mother.

Matt was out of the car within seconds, grabbing his kit, along with a monitor and paediatric bag.

With a jolt, Saffi realised that she recognised the equipment. That was a start, at least. But he was already striding purposefully towards his patient, and Saffi quickly followed him.

Her heart turned over when she saw the small boy lying in the road. He was only six...six years old. This should never be happening.

After a brief conversation with the paramedics, Matt crouched down beside the child. 'How are you doing?' he asked the boy.

The child didn't answer. He was probably in shock. His eyes were open, though, and Matt started to make a quick examination.

'My leg...don't touch my leg!' The boy suddenly found his voice, and Matt acknowledged that with a small intake of breath. It was a good sign that he was conscious and lucid.

'All right, Charlie. I'll be really careful, okay? I just need to find out where you've been hurt, and then I'll give you something for the pain.'

Matt shot Saffi a quick look and she came to crouch beside him. 'He has a fractured thigh bone,' he said in a low voice so that only she could hear. 'He's shivering—that's probably a sign he's losing blood, and he could go downhill very fast. I need to cannulate him, get some fluid into him fast, before the veins shut down.'

He explained to Charlie and his mother what he was going to do. The mother nodded briefly, her face taut, ashen.

Saffi could see that the boy's veins were already thin and faint, but Matt managed to access one on the back of the child's hand. He inserted a thin tube and taped it securely in place, then attached a bag of saline.

The paramedics helped him to splint Charlie's leg, but just as they were about to transfer him to the trolley the boy went deathly pale and began to lose consciousness.

Matt said something under his breath and stopped to examine him once more.

'It could be a pelvic injury,' Saffi said worriedly, and Matt nodded. He wouldn't have been able to detect that through straightforward examination.

'I need to bind his pelvis with a sheet or something. He must have internal injuries—we need to get more fluids into him.'

One of the paramedics hurried away to the ambulance

and came back with one of the bed sheets. Matt and the two men carefully tied it around the child's hips to act as a splint, securing the suspected broken bones and limiting blood loss. Saffi noted all that and moved forward to squeeze the saline bag, trying to force the fluid in faster.

Matt glanced at her, his eyes widening a fraction, but he nodded encouragement. She'd acted out of instinct and he must have understood that.

A minute or two later, the paramedics transferred Charlie to the ambulance, and Matt thrust his car keys into Saffi's hands. 'I'm going with him to the hospital,' he said. 'Do you think you could follow us? I'll need transport back afterwards. Are you still insured to drive?'

She stared at the keys. She'd not driven since the accident, not because she didn't know how but because, for some reason, she was afraid to get behind the wheel. It didn't make sense—her accident had been nothing to do with being in a car.

'Saffi?'

'Y-yes. I'll follow you.' She had to know if the boy was safe.

He left her, and she went to the car, opening the door and sliding into the driver's seat. She gripped the wheel, holding onto it until her knuckles whitened. She couldn't move, paralysed by fear. Then she saw the ambulance setting off along the road, its siren wailing. Charlie was unconscious in there, bleeding inside. His life was balanced on a knife-edge.

Saffi wiped the sweat from her brow and turned the

key in the ignition. She had to do this. Her hand shook as she moved the gear lever, but she slowly set the car in motion and started on the journey to the nearest hospital.

Matt was already in the trauma room when she finally made it to her destination. 'How is he? What's happening?' she asked.

'It's still touch and go. They're doing a CT scan right now.'

'Do you want to wait around to see how he goes on?'

'I do, yes.'

'Okay.' She thought of the boy, looking so tiny as he was wheeled into the ambulance. Tears stung her eyelids and she brushed them away. She was ashamed of showing her emotions this way. Doctors were supposed to be in control of themselves, weren't they?

It had been a mistake for her to come here. She wasn't ready for this.

Matt put his arm around her. 'It'll be a while before we know anything,' he said. 'We could go and wait outside in the seating area near the ambulance bay. They'll page me when they have any news.'

She let him lead the way, and they sat on a bench seat next to a grassed area in the shade of a spreading beech tree.

He kept his arm around her and she was glad of that. It comforted her and made her feel secure, which was odd because in her world she'd only known him for just a few days.

She was confused by everything that was happening and by her feelings for Matt. Her emotions were in chaos.

CHAPTER THREE

'ARE YOU OKAY?' Matt held Saffi close as they sat on the bench by the ambulance bay. 'It was a mistake to bring you here. I shouldn't have put you through all that—it's always difficult, dealing with children.'

He pressed his lips together briefly. 'I suppose I thought coming with me on the callout might spark something in you, perhaps bring back memories of working in A and E.'

'It did, and I'm all right,' she said quietly. 'It was a wake-up call. Seeing that little boy looking so white-faced and vulnerable made me realise I've no business to be hanging around the house feeling sorry for myself.'

'I don't think you've been doing that. You've had a lot to deal with in these last few months, first with your aunt's death and then the head injury coming soon afterwards. Your aunt was like a mother to you, and losing her was traumatic. No one would blame you for taking time out to heal yourself.'

'You'd think I'd remember something like that, wouldn't you?' She frowned. 'But I do keep getting these images of how she was with me, of moments we shared.

The feelings are intense, but then they disappear. It's really bewildering.'

'It's a good sign, though, that you're getting these flashbacks, don't you think? Like I said, you should try not to get yourself too wound up about it. Things will come back to you, given time.'

'Yes.' She thought of the little boy who was so desperately ill, being assessed by the trauma team right now. 'I can't imagine what Charlie's parents must be going through. This must be a desperate time for them. What are his chances, do you think?'

'About fifty-fifty at the moment. He lost a lot of blood and went into shock, but on the plus side we managed to compensate him with fluids and we brought him into hospital in quick time. Another thing in his favour is that Tim Collins is leading the team looking after him. He's a brilliant surgeon. If anyone can save him, he's the man.'

He sent her a thoughtful glance. 'You came up with the diagnosis right away, and knew we had to push fluids into him fast. That makes me feel a bit less guilty about bringing you out here, if it was worth it in the end.'

She gave him a faint smile. 'It was instinctive…but there was no pressure on me at the time. I don't know how I would cope by myself in an emergency situation. There's been a huge hole in my life and it's made me wary about everything. I doubt myself at every step.'

He nodded sympathetically. 'At least it was a beginning.' He stretched his legs, flexing his muscles, and glanced around. 'Shall we go and walk in the grounds for a while? It could be some time before they page us with the results.'

'Okay. That's a good idea. Anything would be better than sitting here, waiting.'

They walked around the side of the hospital over a grassed area where a track led to a small copse of silver-birch trees. There were wild flowers growing here, pinky-white clover and blue cornflowers, and here and there patches of pretty white campion.

Beyond the copse they came across more grass and then a pathway that they followed for several minutes. It led them back to the hospital building and they discovered an area where wooden tables and bench seats were set out at intervals. Saffi looked around and realised they were outside the hospital's restaurant.

It was late afternoon, and there were few people inside the building, and none but themselves outside. They chose a table on a quiet terrace and Saffi sat down once more.

'I'll get us some drinks,' Matt said, and came back a few minutes later with a couple of cups of coffee. 'This'll perk you up a bit,' he murmured. 'All you need is a bit of colour in your cheeks and you'll soon be back to being the girl I once knew.'

'Will I?' She looked at him, her eyes questioning him. 'You don't think she's gone for ever, then?'

He shook his head. 'No, Saffi. The real you is there, under the surface, just waiting to come out.'

He sat beside her and she sipped her coffee, conscious that he was watching her, his gaze lingering on her honey-coloured hair and the pale oval of her face.

After a while, she put down her cup and said thoughtfully, 'How well did you and I know one another?'

He seemed uncomfortable with the question, but he said warily, 'Well enough.'

His smoke-grey glance wandered over the pale gold of her shoulders and shifted to the pink, ripe fullness of her lips. Sudden heat flickered in his eyes, his gaze stroking her with flame as it brushed along her mouth, and despite her misgivings an answering heat rose inside her, a quiver of excitement running through her in response.

He was very still, watching her, and perhaps she had made some slight movement towards him—whatever the reason, he paused only for a second or two longer, never lifting his gaze from her lips, and as he leaned towards her she knew instinctively what he meant to do. He was overwhelmingly masculine, achingly desirable, and she was drawn to him, compelled to move closer, much closer to know the thrill of that kiss. Yet at the same time a faint ripple down her spine urged caution as though there was some kind of hidden danger here, a subtle threat to her peace of mind.

A clattering noise came from inside the restaurant, breaking the spell, and she quickly averted her gaze. She'd wanted him to kiss her, yearned for it, and that knowledge raced through every part of her being. Through all her doubts and hesitation she knew she was deeply, recklessly attracted to him.

She took a moment to get herself together again, and

when she turned to him once more she saw that there was a brooding, intent look about him, as though he, too, had been shaken by the sudden intrusion.

'You didn't really answer my question,' she said softly. '"Well enough" hardly tells me anything. Why are you keeping me in the dark?'

He looked uncomfortable. 'I…uh…I think it's probably better if you remember for yourself—that way, you won't have any preconceived ideas. In the meantime, we can get to know each other all over again, can't we?'

She stared at him in frustration, wanting to argue the point. Why wouldn't he open up to her about this? But his pager went off just then and he immediately braced himself.

'They're prepping Charlie for surgery,' he told her after a moment or two. 'I'll go and find out what came up on the CT scan.'

'I'll go with you.'

'Are you sure you're ready to do this?' He looked at her doubtfully.

'Yes. I'm fine.' She'd now recovered from her earlier bout of tearfulness and she should be more able to cope with whatever lay ahead. Perhaps she just hadn't been ready to face that situation… It was one thing coming back to medicine, but quite another to find herself caught up in the middle of one of the worst possible incidents. No one, not even doctors, wanted to come across an injured child.

'Hi, boss,' the registrar greeted Matt as they arrived back in the trauma unit.

Saffi looked at Matt in astonishment. He was in charge here? That was another shock to her system. No wonder he exuded confidence and seemed to take everything in his stride.

'Hi, Jake. What did they come up with in Radiology?'

Jake showed them the films on the computer screen. 'It's pretty bad, I'm afraid.'

Saffi winced when she saw the images, and Matt threw her a quick glance and said quietly, 'You know what these show?'

She nodded. 'He has a lacerated spleen as well as the leg injury, and there's definitely a fracture of the pelvis.'

'He's lost a lot of blood but he's stable for the moment, at any rate,' Jake said. 'We don't know yet if he'll have to lose the spleen. Mr Collins will take a look and then decide what needs to be done. The boy's going to be in Theatre for some time.' He hesitated. 'You know, there's nothing more you can do here. You'd be better off at home.'

'I know, you're right,' Matt agreed with a sigh. 'Thanks, Jake.'

He walked with Saffi back to the car park a few minutes later. 'You weren't too sure about driving here, were you?' he said. 'How did it go?'

'It was difficult at first, but then it became easier.' She pulled a face. 'I suppose I should have persevered a bit more before getting rid of my car.'

He opened the passenger door for her. 'I suspected there was more to it when you sold your car...some kind of problem with driving. It might not be a bad idea to get yourself some transport now that you've made a start… keep up the good work, so to speak. It would be a shame if you were to lose your nerve again.'

She studied him thoughtfully as he slid behind the wheel and started the engine. Then she said in a faintly accusing tone, 'You did it on purpose, didn't you—giving me the keys? What would have happened if I'd refused? How would you have managed to get home?'

'Same way as always. I'd have cadged a lift back with the paramedics or hailed a taxi. Sometimes the police will drive the car to the hospital for me.' His mouth twitched. 'I was pretty sure you could do it, though. You're not one to give up easily.'

She frowned. 'That makes two trials you've put me through in one day—I suppose I can expect more of this from you? Do you have some sort of interest in me getting back on form?'

He thought about that. 'I might,' he said with a smile. 'Then again…' He frowned, deep in thought for a second or two. 'Perhaps it would be better if…' He broke off.

'If…?' she prompted, but he stayed annoyingly silent, a brooding expression around his mouth and eyes. What was it that he didn't want her to remember? What had happened between them that he couldn't bring himself to share? It was exasperating not being able to bring things to mind in an instant. Would she ever get to know the truth?

An even darker thought popped into her head…he had grown on her this last week or so, but would she still feel the same way about him if she learned what was hidden in their past? Perhaps that was what haunted him.

He parked up at the house, and she left him to go back to the annexe alone. It had been a long, tiring day for her so far, and she needed to wind down and think things through.

'Will you let me know if you hear anything from the hospital?'

'Of course. Though I doubt they'll ring me unless there's any change for the worse. No news is good news, so to speak.'

'Okay.'

She hadn't expected to remember so much of her work as a doctor, but it had started to come back to her when Charlie's life had hung in the balance. What should she do about that? Was she ready to return to work? Would she be able to cope on a day-to-day basis?

Anyway, she wasn't going to decide anything in a hurry. For the moment she would concentrate on getting back to normality as best she could. She would do as her doctor had suggested, and take advantage of her time here in Devon to recuperate, by doing some gardening, or wandering round the shops in town, and exploring the seashore whenever the weather was good.

The very next day she made up her mind to go down to the beach. They were enjoying a few days of brilliant sunshine, and it would have been sheer folly not to make the most of it.

The easiest way to get there from the house was via a

crooked footpath that ended in a long, winding flight of steps and eventually led to a small, beautiful cove sheltered by tall cliffs. She'd been there a couple of times since her arrival here, and she set off again now, taking with her a beach bag and a few essentials…including sun cream and a bottle of pop.

The cove was fairly isolated, but even so several families must have had the same idea and were intent on enjoying themselves by the sea.

She sat down in the shade of a craggy rock and watched the children playing on the smooth sand. Some splashed at the water's edge, while others threw beach balls or dug in the sand with plastic buckets and spades. Her eyes darkened momentarily. This was what Charlie should be doing, enjoying the weekend sunshine with his family.

There'd been no news from the hospital about the little boy, and she'd thought about giving them a call. But she wasn't a relative, and none of the staff at the hospital knew her, so she doubted they would reveal confidential information. She had to rely on Matt to tell her if there was anything she needed to know. He would, she was sure. She trusted him to do that.

She frowned. He was so open with everything else. Why was he so reluctant to talk about their past?

A small boy, dressed in blue bathing trunks, came to stand a few yards away from her. He was about four years old, with black hair and solemn grey-blue eyes, and he stood there silently, watching her. There was an empty bucket in his hand.

She smiled at him and put up a hand to shield her eyes from the sun. 'Hello. What's your name?'

'Ben.'

'I'm Saffi,' she told him. 'Are you having a good time here on the beach? The sand's lovely and warm, isn't it?'

He nodded, but said nothing, still staring at her oddly, and she said carefully, 'Are you all right? Is something bothering you?'

He shrugged his shoulders awkwardly and she raised a questioning brow. 'You can tell me,' she said encouragingly. 'I don't mind.'

'You look sad,' he said.

Ah. 'Do I?' She smiled. 'I'm not really. It's too lovely a day for that, isn't it?'

He nodded, but his expression was sombre, far too wise for a four-year-old.

'Are you sad sometimes?' she asked, prompted by a vague intuition.

He nodded again. 'It hurts here,' he said, putting a hand over his tummy.

Saffi watched him curiously, wondering what could be making him feel unhappy. Being here on the beach and being out of sorts didn't seem to go together somehow.

'Do you feel sad now?' she asked.

He shook his head. 'I did, a bit, 'cos I don't see Daddy every day, like I used to. But it's all right now.'

'Oh. Well, that's good. I'm glad for you. Are you on holiday here with your daddy?'

He shook his head. 'We live here.'

She looked around to see if his father was anywhere nearby, and saw a man just a few yards away, in rolled-up jeans and tee shirt, kneeling down in the sand, putting the finishing touches to a large sandcastle. When he stood up and looked around, Saffi's throat closed in startled recognition.

Matt came towards them. 'What are you up to, Ben? I thought you were coming down to the sea to fill up your bucket. Or have you changed your mind about getting water for the moat?'

Then he looked at Saffi and his eyes widened in appreciation, taking in her curves, outlined by the sun top and shorts that clung faithfully to her body. 'Hi…I wondered if I might see you down here some time.'

She nodded vaguely, but inside she was reeling from this new discovery. Matt had a son? That meant he was married—or at least involved with someone. It was like a blow to her stomach and she crumpled inside. Was this what he'd been trying to keep under wraps? No wonder she'd been guarded about her feelings towards him… her subconscious mind had been warning her off…but weren't those warnings all too late?

Ben was looking at Matt with wide-eyed innocence. 'I do want to finish the moat. I was just talking to the lady.'

'Hmm.' Matt studied him thoughtfully. 'You know what we've said about talking to strangers?'

The boy nodded. 'But she's not a stranger, is she? I know her name. She's Saffi.'

Matt made a wry face, trying unsuccessfully not to smile at that marvellous piece of childish logic.

He shook his head, looking at Saffi. 'I guess I don't need to introduce you to one another. Ben seems to have taken care of all that for me.' He lightly ruffled the boy's hair. 'He's going to be staying with me for a week or so.'

'Oh, I see,' she said slowly, and then with a dry mouth she added quietly, 'I didn't realise you had a child. You didn't say anything about him.'

He raised his brows in surprise. 'You think I have a child? Heavens, no—that's not going to happen any time soon. I'm not planning on getting involved in any deep, long-term relationships.' He frowned. 'Once bitten, as they say…'

Saffi stared at him, feeling a mixture of relief and dismay at his words. He wasn't married. That was something at least. But as to the rest, she didn't know what to think. He'd spoken quickly, without giving the matter much thought, but it was clear his feelings were heartfelt. Once bitten, he'd said. Who had hurt him and made him feel that way?

Matt seemed to give himself a shake to get back on track and said, 'Ben's my nephew, my sister's child. I should have told you right away, but I think I was a little bit distracted with this talking-to-strangers business. I barely took my eyes off him while I finished off the drawbridge, yet he managed to wander off. I could see him, out of the corner of my eye, talking to someone, but you have to be so careful… It can be a bit of a nightmare, taking care of children.'

'Well, yes. I can see that it must be worrying.' She was still caught up in his comment about long-term relationships. So, when he flirted with her it was nothing more than a bit of fun, a light-hearted romance. Of course it was. Why would she have expected anything more? She barely knew him.

At least it was out in the open, though, and she would be on her guard even more from now on. She didn't think she was the sort of woman who would be content with a relationship that wasn't meaningful. Or was she? Her mind was a blank where past boyfriends were concerned.

Matt turned to Ben once more, crouching down so that he was at the boy's level. 'I think you and I need to have another serious chat some time, Ben. Do you remember we talked about strangers?'

Ben nodded.

'That's good. So, what would you say if a stranger came up to you and asked if you'd like a sweet?'

Ben thought about it. 'Um… Yes…please?' he answered in an overly polite voice, and Matt groaned.

'I've a feeling it's going to be a long conversation,' he murmured, getting to his feet. 'Do you want to sort through those pebbles in the other bucket, Ben? See if you can pick out the smallest.'

'Okay.' Ben went to do as Matt suggested.

Saffi smiled. 'How is it that you're looking after him?'

'Gemma's ill—my sister, that is. She hasn't been well for some time, but late last night she rang me and said she was feeling much worse. I went over there and decided she needed to be in hospital. She didn't want to go, and kept saying it was just stress, but I insisted. At the very least, I thought she needed to have tests.'

Saffi sucked in a quick breath. 'I'm sorry. That must have been upsetting—for you and for Ben—for all of you.'

'Yeah, it was a bit of a blow.'

'How has he taken it? He must miss his mother.'

'He's not doing too badly. I explained that she was poorly and needed to rest, and he thinks he's spending time with me so we can have fun together.' He looked at Ben once more. 'Why don't you put some of those pebbles on the wall of the sandcastle, while I talk to Saffi?'

The boy nodded, his eyes lighting up with anticipation. 'Okay.'

'What's wrong with her?' Saffi said, once the boy was absorbed in his new pursuit. 'Do you mind me asking?'

He shook his head. 'No, that's all right. We're not sure what the problem is, exactly. She's been feeling tired and nauseous for a few weeks now, with a lot of digestive problems, and yesterday she was vomiting blood.'

He glanced at Ben, to make sure he couldn't hear. 'That's why I took her to the hospital, so that the doctors can find the source of bleeding and cauterise it. They'll start doing a series of tests from tomorrow onwards to find out what's causing the problem.'

'It's good that your sister can rely on you to take care of things,' Saffi said. 'But how is it going to work out, with you looking after Ben? You have to be on duty at the hospital throughout the week, don't you?'

'Yes, but he'll be at day nursery some of the time, and

for the rest he'll be with a childminder until I'm free to look after him. We'll muddle through, somehow.'

He smiled at her. 'Anyway, it's good to see you here. Do you want to help us finish off this sandcastle? Ben's been nagging me to bring him down here and get on with it since breakfast this morning. Of course, he's not satisfied with plain and simple. The bigger, the better.'

She went over to the castle. 'Wow. It looks pretty good to me.' There were towers and carved windows and walls that surrounded different levels. 'It's fantastic,' she said, and Ben beamed with pleasure at her praise.

She looked at Matt. 'You must have been working on this all afternoon.'

'Pretty much,' Matt agreed. 'There's no slacking with this young man. He knows exactly what he wants.'

She watched the little boy arrange small pebbles on top of the castle's main wall. He did it with absorbed concentration, placing each one carefully.

'Shall I make some steps just here, around the side?' Saffi asked, kneeling down, and Ben nodded approvingly.

Matt knelt down beside her and added some finishing touches to the drawbridge. After a while he sat back on his heels and surveyed his handiwork.

'That's not looking too bad at all,' he mused, wiping the beads of sweat from his forehead with the back of his hand.

Saffi smiled at his boyish satisfaction. 'You look hot. Do you want a drink?'

He nodded and she rummaged in her canvas beach

bag until she found the bottle of pop. 'Here, try some of this.'

He drank thirstily, and when he had finished she offered the bottle to Ben. He took a long swallow and then went back to work with the pebbles.

She glanced at Matt, who was studying the castle once more. 'Has there been any news from the hospital?' she asked, having a quick drink and then putting the bottle back in her bag.

He nodded. 'I rang the hospital just before we left the house. Tim managed to repair Charlie's spleen, and stabilised the pelvis. He'll be non-weight-bearing for a while, and he'll have to wear a spica cast for a few weeks, while the fractures in his leg and pelvis heal, but he should gradually return to his normal activities. He came through the operation all right and Tim thinks he should recover well.'

'I'm so glad about that.' Saffi gave a slow sigh of relief. 'I don't suppose you found out how he is in himself?'

'He's obviously frail and shocked right now, but children are very resilient. They seem to get over things far quicker than we expect.'

He glanced at Ben. 'It all makes me thankful that it didn't happen to my own family. Though I guess I have Gemma to worry about now.'

Kneeling beside him, Saffi laid a comforting hand on his arm. 'You did the right thing, taking her to hospital. I'm sure they'll get to the root of the problem before too long.'

'Yes, I expect so.' He looked at her hand on his arm and overlaid it with his own. His fingers gently clasped hers and his gaze was warm as it touched her face softly. 'You're very sweet, Saffi. It's good to have you here.'

She smiled in response, but they broke away from one another as Ben urged them to look at his creation.

'That's great,' Matt told him. 'I think we can say it's actually finished now, can't we?'

'It's wonderful,' Saffi said.

She sat back and watched Matt and Ben, their heads together, admiring their handiwork.

A tide of warmth ran through her. What was not to love about Matt? She was drawn to him despite her misgivings. He was everything any woman could want... and yet instinct told her she had to steel herself against falling for him.

Didn't she have enough problems to contend with already? He wasn't the staying kind, he'd more or less said so, and the last thing she needed was to end up nursing a broken heart.

CHAPTER FOUR

SAFFI HEARD A rustling sound behind her and turned around to see that Ben had come into the garden. He stood, solemn faced, just a few yards away from her.

'Hello,' she said with a smile. 'You're up and about bright and early. Are you ready for school?'

He nodded, not speaking, but watched as she tended the flowers at the back of one of the borders. It was breakfast-time, but she'd wanted to get on with the work before the sun became too hot.

'I'm putting stakes in the ground so that I can tie up the gladioli,' she told him, guessing that he was interested in what she was doing but unwilling to talk to her. 'See? I've wrapped some twine around the stem.'

He stayed silent but seemed content to stay and watch her as she worked, and she wished there was some way she could bond with him, or at least reach out to him. What could be going on inside his head? Of course, he must be missing his parents. The disruption going on in his family was a lot for a four-year-old to handle.

'Sometimes the flower stems get too heavy and fall over,' she told him, trying to include him in what she was doing, 'or they might bend and break. Tying them like this keeps them standing upright.'

He nodded almost imperceptibly, and they both stood for a while, looking at the glorious display of flowers on show. There were half a dozen different colours, and Saffi was pleased with the end result of her work.

'It's time we were setting off for nursery school, Ben.' Matt came to find his nephew and smiled at Saffi. 'Hi.' His gaze was warm and in spite of her inner warnings her heart skipped a beat as her glance trailed over him.

'Hi.'

He was dressed for work in his role as the man in charge of A and E and the trauma unit, wearing a beautifully tailored suit, the jacket open to show a fine cotton shirt and subtly patterned silk tie.

'It's looking good out here,' he said, glancing around. 'You definitely have green fingers.'

Saffi glanced down at her grimy hands and made a face. 'In more ways than one,' she said with a laugh. 'I suppose I'd better go and clean up. I need to make a trip to the shops to get some food in. The cupboard's bare.'

'Uh-huh. That won't do, will it?' His glance drifted over her, taking in her dark blue jeans and short-sleeved top. There was a glint in his dark eyes. 'We can't have you fading away and losing those delicious curves.'

Her cheeks flushed with heat, but he added on an even note, 'I can give you a lift into the village if you like. But we need to leave in ten minutes.'

'Oh…' She quickly recovered her composure. 'Okay, thanks. I'll be ready in two ticks.'

She hurried away to wash her hands, and met up with Ben and Matt at the front of the house a short time later. They were waiting by the rapid-response vehicle, and as she slid into the passenger seat she asked softly, 'Are you on call again today?'

He nodded. 'Just this morning.'

She was puzzled. 'How does it all fit in with you working at the hospital?'

'Well enough, most of the time. There are some mornings or afternoons when I'm in the office, or attending meetings, rather than being hands on, so to speak, like today, so I fit in outside jobs when I can. Otherwise the call centre has to find other people who are available.'

He smiled. 'At least it means that this morning I can take Ben to nursery, rather than handing him over to Laura, his childminder. His routine's already disturbed, so I want to make things easier for him as best I can. He's been a bit unsettled, with one thing and another.'

'I noticed that,' she said softly. She glanced behind her to see Ben in his child seat, playing with an action figure. 'He's very quiet this morning. I suppose that's understandable, in the circumstances.'

Matt nodded. He parked up outside the day nursery and Saffi went with him to see where Ben would be spending the next few hours. The school was a bright, happy place with colourful pictures on the walls and stimulating puzzles and craft activities set out on the tables for the children.

The staff were friendly and welcoming, and one of

the women took Matt to one side to speak to him while Saffi helped the boy with his coat.

Matt came back to Ben a moment or two later. 'All being well, your daddy will be coming to fetch you at lunchtime,' he said, bending down to give him a hug. Ben's face lit up at the news. 'If he can't make it for some reason, Laura will come as usual. Anyway, have a good time…we'll see you later.'

Saffi and Matt waved as they left the school and went from there to the village store, where Saffi stocked up on essentials like bread, eggs and cheese. Later, as they walked back to the car, she talked to him about Ben's father.

'Does he work away from home a lot of the time?' she asked as they stowed her groceries in the boot alongside all the medical equipment. 'Only, the other day when we were at the beach, Ben told me he feels upset sometimes about not seeing his father so much.'

'Mmm…that's a difficult one. He *is* away a lot of the time…he works for a computer company and goes out to set up systems or resolve problems for business clients in the banking industry or health services. Sometimes it means he has to travel to Scotland, or Wales, or wherever the customer happens to be based. If their systems go down for any reason, he has to sort it out and recover any lost data.'

'Is that why Ben gets anxious—because his father's working life is unpredictable?'

'Possibly. Though he and Gemma have been going through a bad patch lately. That might be something to do with it. They decided to separate, and I think Ben has picked up on the tension. They haven't told him about the split, but most likely he's sensed some of the vibes.'

'I'm sorry. It must be really difficult for everyone.'

'It is, but at least James is home right now. I haven't actually spoken to him, but apparently he called the day nursery to let them know, and he also left a message for Gemma to say he would pick up Ben today—up to now I've tried calling him to let him know that Gemma is ill, but I haven't been able to reach him. I think he must have changed his number.'

'Oh, I see.' She sent him a quick glance. 'It's a bad time for you just now, having to look after Ben and with your sister in hospital. How is she? Is there any news?'

He grimaced. 'Not too much as yet. They're still trying to find what's causing her problems—they've done blood tests, and an endoscopy to check out her stomach and duodenum, and they've taken a biopsy. They're keeping her in hospital because she's very anaemic from loss of blood, and she's lost a lot of weight recently. Obviously, they want to build up her strength.'

'From what you've told me, I'd imagine she must have stomach or duodenal ulcers.'

'Yes, that's right, but the tests have shown they aren't due to any bacterial infection.'

His grey eyes were troubled and she said softly, 'It's worrying for you…if there's anything I can do to help, you only have to ask. I could watch over Ben for you any time you want to go and visit her.'

'Thanks, Saffi.' He squeezed her arm gently. 'I appreciate the offer…but Ben wants to see his mother whenever possible, so I'll probably take him with me.'

She nodded. 'Well, the offer still stands…if there's anything I can do…if you want to talk… A trouble shared is a trouble halved, as they say.' She waited while he closed the boot of the car. 'Do you have any other family?'

'Only my parents, but they don't live locally, and, like me, they're both out at work during the week, so they're not really able to help. And Gemma was desperate to have Ben stay close by.'

'It's good that you were able to look out for him.'

He nodded. 'The other alternative was foster-care, and I didn't want that for him.' His mobile phone trilled, and he quickly took the call, becoming quiet and alert, so she guessed it was the ambulance control centre at the other end of the line.

He cut the call and glanced at Saffi. 'Looks like you get to come along for the ride once again,' he said, a brow lifting questioningly.

She pulled in a quick breath, doubts running through her. Was she up to this? What if it was another child, like Charlie, whose life stood on the brink? Part of her wanted to pull out, to shut herself off from anything medical, but another, more forceful, instinct urged her to face up to her demons.

She nodded. 'Where are we going?' she asked, easing herself into the passenger seat a moment later.

'A riding stables—or, at least, an area close by them. A girl has been thrown from her horse.'

Saffi winced. 'That could be nasty.'

'Yeah.' He hit the blue light and switched on the siren and Saffi clung on to her seat as they raced along the highway, heading away from town towards the depths of the countryside.

A few minutes later, he slowed down as they turned off a leafy lane on to a dirt track that ended at a wide wooden gate, bordered on either side by a rustic fence and an overgrown hedgerow.

Saffi saw a small group of people gathered around a young woman who was lying on the ground. Someone was holding the reins of a horse, and a little further away two more riders stood silently by their mounts. Everyone looked shocked.

Matt stopped the car and removed his jacket, tossing it onto the back seat. He grabbed his medical kit and hurried over to the girl, leaving Saffi to follow in his wake. There was no sign of the ambulance as yet.

'What happened here?' he asked. 'Did anyone see how she fell?'

'The horse reared,' one of the bystanders said, her voice shaking. 'Katie lost her hold on him and fell. Then Major caught her in the back with his hoof as he came down again.'

'Okay, thanks.'

Matt kneeled down beside the injured girl. 'How are you doing, Katie?' he asked. 'Do you have any pain anywhere?'

'In my neck,' she said in a strained voice. 'It hurts if I try to move.'

Saffi could see that she was completely shaken, trau-matised by finding herself in this situation. For Saffi, it was heart-rending, knowing how serious this kind of in-jury could be. If there was a fracture in any of the neck bones, causing spinal-cord damage, this young woman might never walk again.

'All right,' Matt said in a soothing voice. 'It's best if you try to keep as still as possible, so I'm going to put a neck brace on you to prevent any further injury. Once that's in place I'll do a quick examination to make sure everything's all right. Okay?'

'Yes.' The girl was tight-lipped, ashen-faced with pain. She was about seventeen or eighteen, a slender girl with long, chestnut hair that splayed out over the grass.

Saffi helped him to put the collar in place, carefully holding Katie's head while Matt slid it under her neck. Then he fastened the straps and began his examination, checking for any other injuries.

'Shall I start giving her oxygen through a mask?' Saffi asked. Any damage or swelling in the area could eventually deprive the tissues of oxygen and add to the problem.

'Yes, please.' He went on checking the girl's vital signs. 'Heart rate and blood pressure are both low,' he murmured a short time later, glancing at Saffi. 'We need to keep an eye on that. I'll get some intravenous fluids into her to try and raise her blood pressure.'

She nodded. 'She's losing heat, too. Her skin's flushed and dry. We should get her covered up as soon as pos-sible.'

'Yes, it's most likely neurogenic shock. But first we need to get her on to a spinal board. I'll go and fetch it from the car.' He gave a brief smile. 'Last time I saw it, it was underneath a large sack of chicken feed.'

She pulled a face. 'Oops.'

He was soon back with the board, and quickly enlisted a couple of onlookers to help him and Saffi logroll their patient onto the board. 'We need to do this very carefully, no jolting. Is everyone ready?'

On a count of three they gently laid Katie on the board and then Matt covered her with a blanket before securing the straps.

As if on cue, the ambulance finally arrived, and Saffi sighed with relief.

Matt made sure the transfer into the vehicle went smoothly, and once Katie was safely inside, a paramedic stayed beside her to watch over her. The driver closed the doors and then walked round to the cab. Matt spoke to him briefly and a few seconds later Katie was on her way to the hospital.

'I'll follow her and see how she gets on,' Matt said. 'Do you want to come with me or should I call for a taxi to take you home?'

'I'll go with you,' Saffi said quickly. 'I want to know what the damage is.'

'Come on, then. I'll ask the paramedics if they can drop you off at home when they've finished at the hospital.'

He was as worried as she was, she could tell, from the way his mouth was set in a grim line. When they were almost at their destination, though, he relaxed enough to ask, 'How are you coping with all this...coming with me on callouts?'

'All right, I think. It's like stepping into the unknown...I'm a bit scared of what I'll find.'

'But you decided to come along anyway. That must have been hard for you...I could see you were in two minds about joining me.' He sent her a sideways glance. 'So what made you do it in the end?'

'I felt I had to see things through.' Her lips made a flat line. 'After all, this was my career before I fell down the stairs and lost my memory. I need to know if I can go back to it at some point.'

'Do you think that will happen?'

She sighed. 'I don't know. It's one thing to stand to one side and watch, but it's a whole different situation making decisions and holding someone's life in your hands.'

He nodded agreement. 'Yes, I can see how that would be difficult.'

He turned his attention back to the road, pulling up at the hospital a few minutes later. They hurried into the trauma unit.

'Hi, there,' Jake greeted him at the central desk, and smiled at Saffi. 'Are you here to find out about the girl from the riding accident?'

'We are,' Matt said. 'What's been happening so far? Have you been in touch with her parents?'

'They're on their way...should be here in about half an hour. She's been down to X-Ray and right now the neurologist is examining her reflexes. Her blood pressure's still low, so we're giving her dopamine to improve cardiac output.'

'And the heart rate? Has that improved?'

'It's getting better. She's had atropine, two milligrams so far.'

'Good. That's something, at least. Now, these X-ray films—'

'Coming up.' Jake brought up the pictures on the screen and Matt sucked his breath through his teeth.

'That's a C7 fracture. She'll need to go for surgery to get that stabilised. See if Andrew Simmons is available to come and look at her.'

'I will. I think I saw him earlier in his office.'

'Okay. She'll need her pain medication topped up and steroids to bring down the inflammation.'

'I'll write it up. Gina Raines is her specialist nurse. I'll let her know.'

Matt's head went back. 'Gina?'

Saffi frowned. It was clear he was startled by this information for some reason.

'Yes, she generally works at the community hospital, but she transferred over here a couple of days ago on a temporary contract. She's pretty good at the job, from what I've seen.'

'Oh, yes,' Matt said. 'She's certainly well qualified. She was always keen to get on.' His expression was guarded and Saffi wondered what had brought about this sudden change in him. Had he worked with Gina before this? From the sound of things, he knew her fairly well.

'It's all right, Jake,' he said briskly, getting himself back on track. 'I'll go and speak to her myself. Perhaps you could concentrate on chasing up Andrew Simmons.'

'I'll do that.'

Matt turned to Saffi, laying a hand lightly on her elbow. 'Are you okay to go home with the paramedics? They have to go through the village on the way to the ambulance station.'

'Yes, that's fine, as long as they don't mind helping me transfer my groceries from your car.'

'I'm sure they'll be okay with that.'

He seemed concerned about her and Saffi smiled at him. 'Don't worry about me. I know you want to see to your patient and I understand that you're busy.'

He relaxed a little. 'They'll be in the restaurant, getting coffee, I imagine, but I asked them to page me when they're ready to go.'

She walked with him to the treatment bay where Katie was being looked after by a team of doctors and nurses. The girl was still wearing the rigid collar that protected her cervical spine, and she looked frightened, overwhelmed by everything that was happening. A nurse was doing her best to reassure her. Was this Gina?

The nurse's glance lifted as Matt entered the room and there was an immediate tension in the air as they looked at one another.

'Well, this is a surprise,' she said. There was a soft lilt to her voice. She was an attractive woman with green eyes and a beautifully shaped mouth, and dark brown hair that was pinned up at the back in a silky braid. 'It's been quite a while, Matt.'

'It has. I—uh—wasn't expecting to see you here.'

'No. I'm standing in for the girl who went off on maternity leave.'

'Ah.' He cleared his throat, and Saffi guessed he was more than a little disturbed by this meeting. 'So, how's our patient doing?'

'She's very scared.'

'That's only natural.' He walked over to the bedside and squeezed Katie's hand gently. 'Your parents are on their way, Katie. They should be here soon.'

He spoke in a calm, soothing voice, comforting her as best he could and answering her questions in a positive manner. After a while, the girl seemed a little less tense.

Gina looked at him in quiet satisfaction as they walked away from the bedside. 'You were always good with the patients,' she murmured. 'You seem to have the magic touch.'

'Let's hope her faith in me isn't misplaced,' he said, his mouth making a taut line.

Gina glanced at Saffi, and her eyes widened a fraction. 'Saffi. I thought you were based in Hampshire? Are you working here now?'

'Um. No. I'm just visiting.' She was flummoxed for a while after Gina spoke to her. It seemed that the nurse knew her, as well as Matt, and that made her feel more confused than ever. How many more people would she come across that she didn't recognise?

'Saffi's been in an accident,' Matt said, giving the

nurse a strangely intent look. His pager bleeped and he quickly checked it, before adding, 'She has amnesia and she's here to recover.'

'Oh, I'm sorry.'

'It's all right.' Saffi was suddenly anxious to get away, her mind reeling with unanswered questions. Just how well did Matt and Gina know one another? Quite closely, she suspected, from the way Gina looked at him. Would they be getting back together again?

Her mind shied away from the thought. She realised she didn't want to think of Matt being with another woman, and that thought disturbed her and threw her off balance.

'I'd better leave you both to your work,' she murmured. 'I should be going now, anyway.' She turned to Matt. 'Was that the paramedics paging you a moment ago?'

He nodded. 'They're waiting by the desk. I'll take you over to them.'

'No, don't bother. You stay here and look after your patient.'

He frowned. 'If you're sure?'

'I am.'

'Okay, then. Bye, Saffi.'

'Bye.' She nodded to Gina and hurried away. More than ever she felt as though she needed to escape. How was it that Matt had crept into her heart and managed to steal it away?

The paramedics were a friendly pair, making up for the stress of the job they were doing with light-hearted humour. Word of the exchange between Matt and Gina must have travelled fast, because they were chatting about it on the journey home.

'Is she another conquest in the making, do you think?' the driver said with a smile.

His partner nodded. 'I wouldn't be surprised. I don't know how he does it. I could do with a bit of his charisma rubbing off on me.'

They both chuckled, and Saffi kept quiet. Heaven forbid they should see her as yet another woman who had managed to fall for the good-looking emergency doctor. Just how many girls had fallen by the wayside where Matt was concerned?

The paramedics dropped her off at the house and then left, giving her a cheerful wave.

She started on some chores, desperate to take her mind off the image of Matt and Gina being together. It bothered her much more than she liked to admit. She'd wanted to stay free from entanglements, but somehow Matt had managed to slide beneath her defences and now she was suffering the consequences.

Some time later, she glanced through the local newspaper, studying the advertisements for cars. One way or another, she had to steer clear of Matt before she became too deeply involved with him. She could finish up being badly hurt, and she'd been through enough already, without adding that to her troubles. Having her own transport would be a start. But was she ready to get back behind the wheel? That one time she'd driven Matt's car was still seared on her brain.

Around teatime, she went out into the garden to feed the hens. She filled up a bucket with grain from the wooden shed but as she was locking the door a huge clamour started up, coming from the chicken run. Filled with alarm, she hurried over there. Had a fox managed to get in? But hadn't Matt told her there was wire mesh under and around the base of the pen to keep scavengers out? Besides, there were solid walls and fences all around the property.

The hens were squawking, making a huge din, scurrying about, flapping their wings in distress, and she was startled to see that, instead of a fox, it was Ben who was behind the disturbance.

He was running around, shouting, waving his arms and shooing the hens from one end of the compound to the other. How had he managed to get in there? She looked around and saw an upturned plastic flower tub by the side of the gate. He must have climbed on it to reach the door catch.

'Ben! Stop that right now.' Matt strode towards the enclosure as though he meant business.

Ben stood stock-still, his face registering dismay at being caught doing something wrong, swiftly followed by a hint of rebellion in the backward tilt of his head and in the peevish set of his mouth.

Matt opened the door to the run and he and Saffi both went inside.

'I know you think it's fun to get the hens running about like this,' Matt said, 'but they're not like you and me…they could die from fright. You have to be careful around them.'

Ben's brow knotted as he tried to work things out in his head, and Saffi wondered if he actually knew what it meant to die from fright. He certainly knew from Matt's tone of voice that it wasn't a good thing. In the meantime, the hens went on squawking, still panicked.

'I'm sorry about this, Saffi,' Matt said. 'He's been fractious ever since I fetched him from the childminder.'

'It's not your fault.' She frowned. 'I thought he was supposed to be with his father this afternoon?'

'He was, for a while, but apparently James was called away again.'

'Oh, I see.' She made a face. 'That can't have helped.'

'No. Anyway, I'll take him away and leave you to get on.' He turned to Ben and said firmly, 'Come on, young man, we're going back to the house.'

The boy went to him as he was told, but there were tears of frustration in his eyes and Saffi's heart melted. He was obviously upset about his father and over- whelmed at being in trouble, and maybe all he needed was some kind of distraction therapy.

She cut in quietly, 'Perhaps it would help him to learn how to look after the hens instead of scaring them. I could show him how to feed them, if you like.'

Ben looked at him with an anxious expression and Matt smiled, relenting. 'That's a good idea. Thanks, Saffi.' He looked at Ben. 'You know, it's kind of Saffi to do this, so make sure you behave yourself.'

Ben nodded, the tears miraculously gone, and Saffi

showed him how to grab a handful of corn and scatter it about. He watched as the hens started to peck amongst the sand and gravel and giggled when they nudged his feet to get at the grain.

'You're doing really well,' Saffi told him. 'Your dad would be proud if he could see you now.'

'Would he?' He looked at her doubtfully, and then at Matt.

'Oh, yes,' Matt agreed. 'He would. Shall I take your picture? Then you can show him next time you see him.'

'Yeah.' Ben threw down some more grain, showing off and smiling widely at the camera, and Matt snapped him on his mobile phone. He showed him the photo and the little boy grinned in delight.

'I want to show Mummy.' Ben's expression sobered instantly and tears glistened in his eyes once more. 'I want Mummy.' His bottom lip began to tremble.

Matt put an arm around him and gave him a hug. 'I know you do. We'll go and see her at the hospital after tea.'

'We could pick some flowers for her,' Saffi said. 'I think she'd like that, don't you?'

'Yeah.' Ben rubbed the tears from his eyes and looked at her expectantly. 'Can we do it now?'

'Okay. Let me finish up here and we'll find some for you.'

They made sure the hens were contented once more and then Matt locked up and removed the flower tub from the gate while Saffi went with Ben into the walled garden, carrying a trug and scissors.

'I wonder what your mummy would like?' Saffi said, looking around. 'What do you think, Ben?'

'Those ones.' He pointed to a trellis that was covered with delicate sweet-pea blooms, and Saffi nodded.

'That's a good choice, Ben. I think she'll love those.' She started to cut the flowers, frilly pink-edged blooms along with pale violet and soft blues, placing them carefully in the trug on the ground. The four-year-old went down on his knees and put his nose against them, breathing in the scent.

She smiled. 'These were Aunt Annie's favourites. She planted them every year.' She put down the scissors and handed him the basket. 'I think that's enough now. Why don't you take them into the kitchen and I'll find a ribbon to tie round the stems?'

'Okay.' Ben hurried away, taking extra care with his treasure trove.

'You remembered…' Matt was looking at her in wonder, and Saffi stared at him, not knowing what he was talking about. 'Your Aunt Annie,' he prompted, 'planting sweet peas.' She gasped, stunned by the revelation.

She laughed then, a joyful, happy laugh, full of the excitement of new discovery. 'I remember her showing me how to grow them when I was a small child,' she said, suddenly breathless with delight. 'And then we picked them together and made up little wedding baskets for some children who were going to be bridesmaids.' She laughed again, thrilled by the memory and the unlocking of part of her mind that she had thought was gone for ever.

Matt put his arms around her. 'I'm really glad for you, Saffi.' He hesitated, then asked on a cautious note, 'Has it all come back to you?'

She shook her head. 'No, but I do remember living here when I was a child. She was a wonderful woman. She always had time for me and I loved her to bits.' There was sadness with the memory, and as he heard the slight shake in her voice, Matt held her close, knowing what she was going through.

'I think you've absorbed a lot of her qualities,' he said softly. 'You were so good with Ben just now. I'm not sure I would have handled the situation as well as you did. But now you've given him something to look forward to.'

She smiled up at him. 'He's not a bad boy, just over-whelmed with what's going on in his life right now. He's bewildered by what's happening to him. I feel the same way sometimes, so I think I understand some-thing of what he's going through. His world has turned upside down.'

He sighed, gently stroking her, his hand gliding over her back. 'I know. I wish I could make things right for him…and for you. It was great just now to see you laugh. It lights up your face when you do that,' he said hus-kily, 'and when you smile, I'm helpless… I tell myself I must keep away, and not go down that road but, no matter how much I try to hold back, I just want to kiss you…I'm lost…'

Inevitably, the thought led to the action, and slowly he bent his head and brushed her lips with his. It was a gentle, heart-stopping kiss that coaxed a warm, achingly sweet response from her. As her lips parted beneath his, he gave a ragged groan as though he couldn't stop himself, and he held her tight, drawing her up against him so that her soft curves meshed with his long, hard body and her legs tangled with his muscular thighs.

She ran her hands over him, loving the feel of him. Elation was sweeping through her, the ecstasy of his kisses sending a fever through her blood and leaving her heady with desire—a desire that seemed altogether familiar all at once. She needed him, wanted him.

Had she been wrapped in his arms this way at another time? Her feelings for him were so strong... She loved being with him this way, feeling the thunder of his heartbeat beneath her fingers—could it be that she simply couldn't help falling for him? He'd been so caring, so supportive and understanding of her. Or was there more to it...had she felt this way for him long before this, before her memory had been wiped out?

'You're so beautiful, Saffi,' he whispered, his voice choked with passion. 'It's been so tough, being with you again after all this time, longing to hold you...and yet...I just can't help myself...'

He broke off, kissing her again, his hands moving over her, tracing a path along her spine, over the rounded swell of her hip, down the length of her thigh. It felt so good to have him touch her this way. It felt right...as though this was how it should be.

Her hand splayed out over his shoulder, feeling the strength beneath her palm. 'I want you, too,' she said. She ached for him, but her mind was suddenly spinning with unanswered questions. 'What happened to us, Matt? After all this time, you said…were we together back then?'

A look of anguish came over his face. 'In a way,' he said.

'In a way…?' She broke away from him, looking at him in bewilderment. 'What do you mean? What kind of answer is that?'

'I can't…' He seemed to be waging some kind of inner battle, struggling to get the words out, and finally he said in a jerky, roughened voice, 'I can't tell you how it was. I'm sorry, but…' he sucked in a deep breath '…I think this is something you need to remember for yourself.'

His eyes were dark with torment. 'I shouldn't have kissed you. I don't want to take advantage of you, Saffi… and perhaps for my own self-preservation I should have held back. I should have known better.'

She stared at him in bewilderment. What did he mean when he talked about self-preservation? What was so wrong in them being together—was he so determined against commitment? What was it he'd said before— *once bitten*? Had he been so badly hurt in the past that he didn't want to risk his heart again? But as she opened her mouth to put all these questions to him, his phone began to ring.

At the same time Ben came out of the house, looking indignant. 'I thought we were going to the hospital to see Mummy?' he said crossly. 'You've been ages.'

Matt braced his shoulders. 'We'll go soon,' he told the little boy.

'Do you promise?'

'I promise.' He looked at Saffi and held up the phone, still insistently ringing. 'I'm sorry about this,' he said on a resigned note. 'It might be about the girl in the riding accident.'

'It's all right. Go ahead.' She was deeply disappointed and frustrated by the intrusion, but she took Ben's hand and started towards the house.

The moment of closeness had passed. He might not be forthcoming about what had gone on between them before, but whatever his reasons one thing was for sure... it was much too late now for her to guard against falling for him. She had so many doubts and worries about him, but he'd grown on her and she didn't want to imagine life without him. She was already in love with him.

He pressed the button to connect his call. 'Hello, Gina,' she heard him say, and her heart began to ache.

CHAPTER FIVE

'CAN I DO that?' Ben watched Saffi as she picked runner beans, carefully dropping them one by one into a trug. It was the weekend and the sun was shining, and the only sounds that filled the air were birdsong and the quiet drone of bees as they went about their business. A warm breeze rippled through the plants, making the leaves quiver.

'Of course you can. Here, let me show you how to do it. We snap them off where the bean turns into stalk— like this, see?' He nodded and she added, 'Why don't you try picking some of the lower ones and I'll do these up here?'

'Okay.'

They worked together amicably for a while, with Ben telling her about his visits to the hospital. 'Mummy's still poorly,' he said. 'She's got lots of…um…acid…inside her, and it's hurting her. They don't know why she's got it.'

'I'm sorry to hear that, Ben. But the doctors are looking after her, and I'm sure they'll soon find out what's causing her to be poorly.'

'Yeah.' His eyes grew large. 'Uncle Matt says they're going to take some pictures of inside her tummy.'

'That's good. That should help them to find out what's wrong.' Saffi guessed he meant they were going to do a CT scan. She winced inwardly. That sounded as though they suspected something quite serious was going on.

'Hi, Saffi.' Matt came to join them in the garden, and immediately she felt her pulse quicken and her stomach tighten. He was dressed in casual clothes, dark chinos and a tee shirt in a matching colour, and it was easy to see why women would fall for him. His biceps strained against the short sleeves of his shirt and his shoulders were broad and powerful. He looked like a man who would take care of his woman, protect her and keep her safe.

'Hi.' She tried to shut those images from her mind, but even so her heart turned over as she recalled the meeting between him and the nurse. They'd known each other for a long time, and from the tension that had sparked between them she guessed there was still a good deal of charged emotion on the loose.

'It's a beautiful day,' she said, trying to get her thoughts back onto safer ground. 'Do you have plans for today, or are you on call?'

He shook his head. 'I don't have any plans. It's not really possible to make any while I'm looking after Ben.' He sent her a thoughtful, hopeful glance. 'I suppose we could all go down to the beach after breakfast, if you'd like to come with us?'

'Yay!' Ben whooped with excitement. 'Come with us, Saffi.'

Saffi smiled at the four-year-old. He hadn't said a lot to her over these last few days, being quiet and intro-spective, but if he wanted her to go with them, that was a heartening sign. It made her feel good inside to know that he had warmed to her.

'I'd like that,' she said. She sent Matt a questioning glance. 'What would you be doing if you didn't have to look after Ben? How do you usually spend your week-ends?' She didn't know much about his hobbies or inter-ests, but from the looks of him he must work out quite a bit at the gym.

He shrugged. 'Sometimes I swim—in the sea, or at the pool—or I might play squash with a friend. I go to the gym quite often. On a day like this, when there's a breeze blowing, a group of us like to go kite-surfing at a beach a bit further along the coast. There's a good southerly wind there and a decent swell.'

'Kite-surfing? I'm not sure if I know what that is.'

'You go out on the sea on a small surfboard, and with a kite a bit like a parachute. The wind pulls you along. It's great once you've mastered the skill.'

Her mouth curved. 'It sounds like fun. Why don't you join your friends? I'll look after Ben on the beach. We can watch the surfing from there. What do you think, Ben?'

'Yeah.' He was smiling, looking forward to the trip.

Matt frowned. 'I can't do that. It's too much to ask of you.'

'No, it's fine, really.' She started to move away from the vegetable garden, but at the same time Ben went to Matt to tug on his trousers and claim his attention.

'I want to see the kites...please, Uncle Matt,' Ben pleaded.

Saffi sidestepped him, trying to avoid a collision, and caught her heel against one of the bean canes.

'Ouch!' She felt a stab of pain as she untangled her foot from the greenery.

'What is it? Have you twisted your ankle?' Matt looked at her in concern, reaching out to clasp her arm as she tried to look behind her at her calf.

She shook her head. 'No. It's a bee sting.'

'Come into the house. I'll have a look at it.' He turned to Ben, who was watching anxiously. 'She'll be fine, Ben. Bring the trug, will you? Can you manage it?'

'Yes, I'm strong, see?' The little boy picked up the basket and followed them into the house.

'Sit down.' Matt showed her into the kitchen and pulled out a chair for her at the table. He reached for a first-aid kit from a cupboard and brought out a pair of tweezers. 'Let's get that sting out. Put your leg up on this stool.'

She did as he suggested. She was wearing cropped cargo pants, and he crouched down and rolled them back a little to expose the small reddened, inflamed area where the bee had stung her. Then he carefully pulled out the sting with the tweezers. Ben watched every move, his mouth slightly open in absorbed concentration.

'Okay, now that's out, we'll get something cold on the leg to help take down the swelling.' He fetched a bag of frozen peas from the freezer and laid it over the tender area. 'Are you all right?'

'I'm fine.' She made a wry face. 'It's not a good start to my beekeeping, is it?'

He smiled. 'I expect you disturbed it. They don't usually sting if you're calm with them and keep your movements slow. When you're working with the hives it might help if you go to them between ten o'clock and two in the afternoon, when most of the bees are busy with the flowers…and make sure you always wear protective clothing. That's what Annie told me.'

He looked at her leg, lifting the frozen plastic bag from her. 'That's not quite so inflamed now. I'll rub some antihistamine cream on it, and it should start to feel easier within a few minutes.'

'Thanks.' She watched him as he smoothed the cream into her leg, his head bent. He was gentle and his hands were soothing, one hand lightly supporting her leg while he applied cream with the other. She could almost forget the sting while he did that. She studied him surreptitiously. His black hair was silky, inviting her to run her fingers through it.

'How are you doing?' He lifted his head and studied her, and she hastily pulled herself together. She felt hot all over.

'I'll be okay now. Thanks.'

'Good.' He held her gaze for a moment or two as though he was trying to work out what had brought colour to her cheeks, and then, to her relief, he stood up. 'Do you want to stay and have breakfast with us, and then we'll head off to the beach? I'm not sure what we're having yet. Toast and something, maybe.'

'That sounds good.' She straightened up and made herself think about mundane things. It wouldn't do her any good to think about getting close up and personal with Matt. Look what had happened last time. He was fighting his own demons, and she was worried about all the other women who might try to take her place.

'I could take Ben with me to collect some eggs. How would that be?' She stood up.

'Dippy eggs and toast soldiers!' Ben whooped again and licked his lips in an exaggerated gesture. 'I love them.'

'Sounds good to me,' Matt agreed. 'But are you sure you don't want to rest your leg for a bit longer?'

'I'll be fine. Why don't you ring your friend and make arrangements to do some kite-surfing? We'll be back in a few minutes.'

She collected a basket from her kitchen and took Ben with her to the hen coop. There she lifted the lid that covered the nesting boxes and they both peered inside.

'I can see two eggs,' he said happily, foraging amongst the wood shavings. 'And there's some more.' He looked in all the nest boxes, carefully picking out the eggs and laying them in the basket. He counted them, pointing his finger at each one in turn. 'There's six.'

'Wow. We did well, didn't we?' Saffi closed the lid on the coop and made everything secure once more.

'Let's go and wash these and then we'll cook them for breakfast.'

'Yum.' Ben skipped back to the house, more animated than she'd seen him in a while.

Over breakfast they talked about kite-surfing for a while, and about how Saffi was coping with the day-to-day running of the property.

'It's fine,' she said. 'It's quite easy once you get into a routine—but, then, I'm not going out to work at the moment, so that makes a big difference.'

Thinking about that, she looked over to Ben. Keeping her voice low she said, 'At least you must be able to see your sister every day, with working at the hospital. How is she? Have they managed to find out what's causing her problems? Could it be anything to do with stress, with the marriage problems, and so on?'

'It's always possible, I suppose. But they're still doing tests—she'll be going for a CT scan on Monday.'

'It must be a worry for you. Do you manage to get together with your parents to talk things through?'

He nodded. 'They've been coming over here to visit her as often as they can. I think my mother will have Ben to stay with her next weekend.'

'That should give you a bit of a break, at least, and I expect Ben will look forward to staying with his grandmother for a while.'

She glanced at the boy, who was placing the empty top piece of shell back onto his egg. He was getting ready to bang it with his spoon.

'Humpty Dumpty,' he said, and they both smiled.

Still dwelling on news from the hospital, Saffi asked, 'Have you heard anything more about the girl who fell from her horse? How's she doing?'

'She's had surgery to stabilise the neck bones, and she's on steroids to bring down the inflammation, as well as painkillers. They'll try to get her up and about as soon as possible to make sure she makes a good recovery. I think she'll be okay. She's young and resilient and she has a lot of motivation to get well again.'

'That's a big relief.'

'Yes, it is.' He seemed pensive for a second or two, and Saffi wondered what was going through his mind.

She glanced at him and said tentatively, 'At the hospital, you seemed quite surprised to see the nurse...Gina. I had the feeling...were you and she a couple at one time?'

Perhaps they still were, or maybe he was planning to resume their relationship... Her mind shied away from the thought.

His mouth flattened. 'We dated for a while.'

'Oh.' She absorbed that for a moment or two. Wasn't it what she had expected? 'Did something happen to break things up? I suppose you moved to different parts of the country?' And now they were reunited once more in Devon...what was there to stop them taking up where they had left off? A shiver of apprehension ran down her spine.

'Gina wanted to take things to a more serious level.' He grimaced. 'I wasn't looking for anything more than a fun time.'

She winced inwardly. Was this the way he treated all

women? Hadn't he admitted as much? As far as she and Matt were concerned, at least he'd had the grace to say he didn't want to take advantage of her.

'That must have been upsetting for her.'

'Yes, I guess it was.'

She frowned. She couldn't see him simply as a man who played the field without any consideration for the feelings of the girls he dated. But if he did, there must surely be a reason for his behaviour. She didn't want to see him as a man who was only interested in seducing women with no thought for the consequences.

They finished breakfast and cleared away the dishes, and Matt started to get his kite-surfing gear together.

'I hope you're all right with this,' he said. 'We're usually on the water for about an hour.'

'I can keep Ben amused for that long, I'm sure.' She smiled. 'Are we about ready to go? I think the waiting's too much for him. He's running around like a demented bee.'

Matt laughed, and a few minutes later he crammed his kite and small surfboard into the back of the rapid-response car and they set off.

'How can you answer an emergency call if you're out on the water?' she asked with a quizzical smile as he drove along the coast road.

'I can't. I'd have to turn them down, and ask them to find someone else to go in my place, but if anything should happen when I'm back on dry land I'll be prepared. Usually I get to enjoy my weekends, but you never know.'

They went a few miles down the road until they arrived at the surfers' beach, a sandy cove, bound by rugged cliffs that were covered with lichens and here and there with moor grass and red fescue.

Matt parked the car and Saffi looked out over the sea as he changed into his wetsuit. He was wearing swimming shorts under his clothes, but it was way too distracting, seeing his strong, muscular legs and bare chest with its taut six-pack. 'From the looks of those people surfing, it must be an exhilarating experience,' she said.

'It is,' Matt agreed. 'If you're interested, I could teach you how to do it—just as soon as we get a day on our own. Do you do any water sports?'

'Um…I've a feeling I do. I know I can swim, anyway, and I think I might like to learn kite-surfing. It's mostly men who do the sport, though, isn't it?'

'Not necessarily. A lot more women are getting into it nowadays. You'd start with a trainer kite and learn simple techniques first of all.' He looked at her expectantly and she nodded.

She was getting her confidence back now, feeling stronger day by day, and maybe it was time to accept some new challenges.

'Maybe I'd like to try,' she said, and he gave her a satisfied smile. She breathed in the salt sea air. It was good to be with him out here, and to look forward to more days like this, but didn't she know, deep down, that she was playing with fire? She was getting closer to him all the time, when the sensible thing would be to keep her distance. It was quite clear he wasn't looking for any serious involvement.

He introduced her to his friends and she and Ben watched from the beach as they went out onto the water. Saffi walked along the sand with the contented little boy, helping him to collect shells in a plastic bucket, looking up every now and again to see the surfers wheeling and diving, letting the wind take them this way and that.

Ben kicked off his shoes and splashed in the waves that lapped at the shore, while Saffi kept a close eye on him, and then they walked back to the base of the cliff where he could dig in the sand.

She saw the surfers moving over the sea at a fast pace, some of them lifted up by the kites from the surface of the waves, skilfully controlling their movements and coming back down again to ride the water. The wind was getting up now, gusting fiercely, and she rummaged in her beach bag for a shirt for Ben.

'Here, put this on. It's getting a bit chilly out here.'

He stopped digging for a while to put on the shirt and then he gazed out at the sea. 'I can't see Uncle Matt,' he said. 'He's too far away.'

'There are two of them in black wetsuits...I'm not sure, but I think that might be him coming in to the—' She broke off, clasping a hand to her mouth in horror as she saw one of the surfers lifted up by a sudden squall. Was it Matt? His kite billowed, the fierce wind dragging him swiftly towards the cliffside so that he was powerless to do anything to stop it. He was hurtling towards the craggy rock face at speed, and Saffi's stomach turned over in sheer dread. As she watched, he hit the jagged rocks near the foot of the cliff and crumpled on to the sand below.

She saw it happen with a feeling of terror. Was it Matt? It couldn't be Matt...she couldn't bear it.

She sprang to her feet. 'Ben, come with me,' she said urgently. 'That man's hurt and I have to help him. We need to get the medical kit from the car.'

He didn't argue but left his bucket and spade behind as they hurried up the cliff path to the car. 'Is it Uncle Matt?' he asked.

'I don't know, sweetheart.' She rummaged in her bag for her phone and called for an ambulance.

'Will you make him better?'

She gently squeezed his hand. 'I'll do everything I can. But you must stay with me, Ben. You can't wander off. I need to know you're safe. Promise me you'll stay close by me.'

'I promise.'

'Good boy. It might not be very nice to see the man that's hurt, so you'll probably need to look away.' Heaven forbid it should turn out to be Matt. She studied him. 'Okay?'

He was solemn-faced, taking in the enormity of the situation. 'Okay.'

She whipped open the boot of the car, thankful that Matt had left the keys with her. She pulled out the heavy medical backpack and the patient monitor and then locked up the car once more and hurried back down the path as fast as she could go, with Ben by her side.

They had to make their way carefully over rocks to get to the injured man and all the time she was praying that it wasn't Matt who was lying there. Whoever it was, he was screaming with pain. A small crowd had gathered around him and she said, 'Let me through, please. I'm a doctor.'

People moved aside and she saw that two lifeguards were already by the man's side. One of them, white-faced, said quietly, 'His foot's twisted round at an odd angle. It's like it's been partly sheared off.'

Saffi pulled in a quick breath. Not Matt, please don't let it be Matt.

'I'll look at him,' she said, shielding Ben from what was going on. 'Would one of you keep an eye on the little boy for me?' She glanced around. 'Perhaps he'd be better over there, out of the way, but where I can still see him.' She pointed to a sheltered place in the lee of the cliff where there was enough sand for him to dig with his hands.

'Sure. I'll do it.'

'Thanks.' She looked down at the kite-surfer and a surge of relief washed through her as she realised it wasn't Matt lying there. It was his friend, Josh. She laid down her pack and knelt beside him.

'Josh, I'm a doctor…I'm going to have a look at you and see if I can make you more comfortable before we get you to hospital. Okay?'

'Okay.' He clamped his jaw, trying to fight the pain, and Saffi went through her initial observations. The foot was purple, with no great blood loss, and he was able to wiggle the toes on his other foot, as well as move his leg.

She didn't think there was any spinal injury but she needed to take precautions all the same, so she asked the lifeguard to help her put a cervical collar around Josh's neck.

Josh's pulse was very fast and his blood pressure was high, most likely because of the excruciating pain. That was going to make it difficult to move him. He might also have other, internal injuries, so the best thing to do would be to administer pain relief.

She asked both lifeguards to help her. 'I'm going to give him drugs to reduce the pain. As soon as I've given him the medication, we'll have to carefully roll him on to his back and set him up with an oxygen mask. Are you all right with that?'

'Yeah, that's okay.'

She glanced at Ben to make sure he was staying put, and then prepared to go on with the procedure. Thankfully, it wasn't likely that he could see much of what was going on, while three people were gathered around Josh. She made sure Josh was as comfortable as possible, looping the oxygen mask over his head.

There was a movement on the periphery of the crowd and she saw that Matt had gone to stand with Ben. She looked at him and he gave her a nod of support.

At the same time, the ambulance siren sounded in the distance, getting nearer.

'Thanks for your help,' she said to the lifeguards as she connected the oxygen cylinder to the tube. 'One last thing…I need one of you to help me get his foot back into the proper position.' If they didn't do that, the circulation could fail and the foot would be useless.

One of the lifeguards hesitantly volunteered. 'I don't know what to do,' he said.

'It'll be all right,' she said, reassuring him. 'I'll talk you through it. We need to give it a tug.'

He swallowed hard, but a few minutes later the foot pinked up, and she could feel that the pulses were present.

She sat back on her heels. The paramedics would help with splinting the foot and getting Josh onto a spinal board. Her work was almost done.

Matt came over to her, holding Ben by the hand, as they transferred his friend to the ambulance a short time later. He'd rolled down the top half of his wetsuit and Saffi couldn't take her eyes off him. He was hunky, perfectly muscled, his chest lightly bronzed. Her heart began to thump against her rib cage and her mouth went dry.

Together, they watched the ambulance move away, and as the crowd dwindled and people returned down the path to the beach Matt drew her to him, putting his free arm around her.

'You were brilliant,' he said. 'I thought about coming over to you to help, but I could see you had everything under control, the whole time. You were amazing. How did it feel?'

'Feel?' She stared at him blankly for a moment, not understanding what he was saying, and then realisation came to her in a rush. Without any conscious thought she'd acted like a true A and E doctor.

'I didn't think about what I was doing,' she said, her eyes widening. 'All I know is I was terrified it might be you who was injured, and I was desperate to make sure you were all right. I couldn't think beyond that. The adrenaline must have taken over.'

'That's my girl.' He hugged her close and kissed her swiftly on the mouth.

His girl? Her heart leapt and she returned his kiss with equal passion, a fever beginning to burn inside her. How did he manage to do this to her every time, to make her want him more than anything, more than any other man?

Where had that thought come from? She didn't remember any other man in her life before this. There must have been, surely? But somehow she was certain that Matt was the one man above all who could stir her senses and turn her blood to flame.

Ben started tugging at Matt's wetsuit. 'Can we go down to the beach? I want to make another sandcastle.'

Matt gave a soft groan and reluctantly broke off the kiss. 'Perhaps I should never have started that,' he said raggedly. 'Wrong place, wrong time.' He frowned. 'It's always going to be like that, isn't it?' he added with a sigh. 'I have to keep telling myself I must stay away, but when I'm with you it's so hard to resist.'

And she should never have responded with such eagerness, Saffi reflected wryly. She knew what she was getting into, and going on his record so far it could only end in sorrow, so why couldn't she keep her emotions firmly under lock and key?

CHAPTER SIX

'HAVE YOU THOUGHT any more about going back to work in A and E?' Matt asked. He'd popped home from the hospital to pick up his laptop, and Saffi was glad to see him, and even more pleased that he'd stopped to chat for a while. She missed him when he wasn't around.

It was lunchtime and she was hosing down the chicken run, a chore she did once a week to make sure the birds' living quarters were scrupulously clean. The hens were out on the grass, exploring the pellets of food she'd scattered about.

Matt seemed keen to know what she planned to do workwise, and she guessed it was because he cared enough to want her to be completely well again. Being able to do the job she'd trained for was a big part of that recovery process.

'I think it would do you good to go back to working in a hospital,' Matt said. 'It could help to bring back some memories.'

She nodded. 'I've been thinking the same thing. I'm just not sure I'd cope with the responsibility—what if I've forgotten some of the techniques I knew before?'

'I know it would be a huge step for you after you've spent the last few months getting yourself back on track, but you did so well looking after Josh—I think you proved yourself then.'

'Maybe.' She was hesitant. Was she really ready for it? He seemed to have a lot of faith in her.

'How is Josh?' she asked, switching off the hose and laying it on the ground. 'His foot was in a pretty bad state, wasn't it?'

'Yes, but he went up to Theatre and Andrew Simmons pinned it with plates and screws, and did a bone graft. It'll take a while to heal, and he'll need physiotherapy, but I think he'll be all right eventually.' He gave her a look of new respect. 'You saved his foot, Saffi. If you hadn't restored the circulation he could have been looking at an amputation.'

'I'm just relieved that he's all right.' She was thoughtful for a second or two. 'One thing I'll say—it's definitely put me off kite-surfing. Are you sure you want to go on doing it? I was worried sick when I thought you might have been hurt.'

'Were you? I'm glad you care about me.' He ran his hands down her arms in a light caress. 'I understand how you feel about trying it out. That's okay. And as for the other—I'm always careful to avoid going close to cliffs or rocks. You don't need to worry about me.'

'That's a relief.'

He studied her briefly. 'So what do you think about going back to work?'

'I don't know. Perhaps I could do it...but I always

thought I would know when the time was right because I'd have recovered all of my memories. It doesn't seem to be happening that way, though, does it?'

'Amnesia can be strange,' he murmured, 'but, actually, you've been doing really well. You've remembered your aunt and your career, and all the time, day by day, you're getting small flashes of recall. Perhaps by going back to your job things will begin to come back to you more and more.' He shooed a hen out of the flower border, where she'd been trying to eat one of the plants. 'Go on, Mitzi, back with the others.'

'You could be right. I don't know why it matters so much to me...but I feel...it's like I'm only half a person.' She looked at him in despair, and he took her into his arms.

'I can't bear to see you looking so forlorn,' he said. 'You mustn't think like that—anyway, you look pretty much like a whole person to me,' he added in a teasing voice. 'So much so that I think about you all the time...I can't get you out of my mind. You're beautiful, Saffi... and incredibly sweet. Look how you coaxed Ben to come out of himself.'

He gave her a gentle squeeze, drawing her nearer, and his words came out on a ragged sigh. 'It's getting more and more difficult for me to keep my resolve. Every time I look at you I want to show you just how much I want you.'

Having his arms around her was a delicious temptation but she couldn't give in to it, could she? Much as she wanted to believe every word he said, she had to make a strong effort to resist. At least, she had to do better than she'd managed up to now.

'Hmm…' She looked into his smoke-grey eyes. 'From what I've heard, that's what you say to all the girls.'

He pressed a hand to his heart as though she'd wounded him. 'It's not true. Would I do that? Would I?'

'I think that's open to debate,' she murmured.

He gave her a crooked smile. 'You're gorgeous, Saffi, and that's the truth, and I feel great whenever I'm with you. I have to keep pinching myself to believe that I'm actually living right next door to you.'

He was saying all the things she wanted to hear, but did she really want to end up as just another conquest? She couldn't get it out of her head what the paramedics had said. He had a way with women.

'You certainly do live next door—and that's another thing about you that confuses me,' she commented on a musing note, trying to ease herself away from him. 'I still haven't figured out why my aunt would leave part of the house to you. It doesn't make any sense to leave a house to be shared by two people who aren't related.'

She rubbed her fingers lightly over her temples in a circling motion to get rid of a throbbing ache that had started up there. Having him so close just added to her problems. She couldn't think straight.

'It's just another of those mysteries that I can't solve…' she murmured, 'but perhaps one day I'll get to the bottom of it. At the moment my mind's like a jigsaw puzzle with lots of little bits filled in.'

He became serious. 'I'm sure things will come back

to you if you start to live the life you once had. I mean it. Going back to work at the hospital could be the best thing for you. I need another doctor on my team, and you would be perfect. You could work part time if it suits you—in fact, that would probably be the best option to begin with.'

'You need someone? You're not just trying to find a job for me?'

'We're desperately short of emergency doctors. I'd really like you to say yes, Saffi, not just for me but also for your own well-being. We'll get clearance for you to work again from the powers that be, and maybe arrange for someone to work with you for a while. I'd keep an eye on you to begin with until you get your confidence back.'

He looked so sincere she knew he would watch over her, and part-time work did seem like the ideal solution for her at the moment. It would give her the best of both worlds and allow her time to adjust.

She swallowed hard. 'Okay,' she said. 'I'll do it.'

'Yay!' He swooped her up into his arms once again and kissed her firmly, a thorough, passionate kiss that left her breathless and yearning for more.

'That's wonderful, Saffi.' He looked at her, his grey eyes gleaming, his mouth curved in a heart-warming smile. 'We should celebrate. Let me take you out to dinner this evening.'

She smiled back at him. 'I'd like that,' she said, 'except...' she frowned '...I'm expecting a visitor at around nine o'clock. He's bringing some stuff I left behind in Hampshire—a few books, my coffee-maker, glassware, things like that. My flatmate has been looking after them for me, but Jason offered to bring them here. Apparently he's coming to Devon to take a few days' holiday.'

Matt frowned. 'Jason? You know this man? I thought you didn't remember anyone from where you lived?'

'No, I don't know him. I mean, I did, apparently, according to my flatmate. She's the only one I recalled after the accident, but even that was just bits and pieces that came back to me before I left Hampshire. Jason's a complete blank in my mind.'

'It seems odd that he's coming over so late in the evening?'

'I suppose it is, but he told Chloe he has to work today. He'll head over here as soon as he's finished.'

'That makes some kind of sense, I suppose.' He was still doubtful, a brooding look coming into his eyes as though he was already weighing up Jason as some kind of competition. His dark brows drew together. 'He must be really keen to see you if it can't wait till morning. Did your flatmate tell you anything about him?'

She could see he was suspicious of the man and his motives. 'No, she didn't, not really…not much, anyway. She mentioned something about us dating a few times. I remember he came to see me when I was in hospital, but I was getting distressed whenever I had visitors—they were all strangers to me and I was a bit overwhelmed by everything that was happening to me. I think the doctors advised her to let me remember things in my own time.' A feeling of unease washed through her. 'I feel bad about it…all those people I was supposed to know…'

'It wasn't your fault, Saffi.' He held her tight. 'Look, how about this—we could go for an early dinner. What do you think? I really want to spend some time with you. I'll make sure you're back here in time to meet up with this Jason...' he pulled a face '...even though I'd rather you weren't going to see him.' His eyes darkened. 'I don't like the idea of him taking up where you left off.' Once again, he was at war with himself. 'I hate the thought of you dating someone else.'

'I'm not dating him. I don't even know him.' She nodded thoughtfully. 'An early dinner sounds like a good compromise. But what will you do about Ben...or will he be coming with us? I don't mind, if that's what you want.'

He shook his head. 'His father's going to look after him. He's back from sorting out the latest crisis, and he says he's going to stay home for a few days.'

'Oh, that's good news.' She smiled. 'Ben will be really happy to see him.'

'Yeah. Let's hope he doesn't get unsettled again when James has to leave.'

She winced. 'You're right, he's really come out of himself this last couple of weeks. Do you think James will take him to see Gemma in hospital?'

'He said he would. He wants to know the results of the CT scan they're doing.'

Of course...they would be doing the scan today. Matt had told her about it. He must be worried sick about what it might reveal.

He checked his watch. 'I have to go. It's almost time

I was back on duty. I'll see you later. Dinner for about seven o'clock? Would that be all right?'

She nodded. 'I'll look forward to it.'

'Good. I'll book a table.'

It was only after he'd left for work that she realised she'd done it again—that she'd agreed to spend time with him when she should be putting up some barriers between them. Did she really want to end up like Gina, still hankering after him years later, when their relationship had run its course? And how would she get on with Gina if they had to work together? Had she made a mistake in agreeing to it?

She shook her head. It was done now, and she may as well throw caution to the wind and look forward to the evening.

What should she wear? After she'd showered and started her make-up later on in the day, she hunted through her wardrobe and picked out a favourite wine-coloured dress, one that she'd brought with her from Hampshire. It was sleeveless, with a V-shaped neckline and pleated bodice, a smooth sash waist and a pencil-line skirt. She put the finishing touches to her make-up, smoothing on a warm lip colour and adding a hint of blusher to her cheeks.

When Matt rang the doorbell at half past six, she was finally ready.

'Hi,' she said. 'I wasn't sure you'd make it here on time. I know how things can be in A and E. It isn't always easy to get away.'

'I handed over to my registrar.' He gazed at her, his

eyes gleaming in appreciation as he took in her feminine curves, outlined by the dress, and her hair, which was a mass of silky, burnished curls. 'You look lovely, Saffi. You take my breath away—you're the girl of my dreams.'

Her cheeks flushed with warm colour at the compliment. He looked fantastic. He must have showered and changed as soon as he had got home from work because his black hair was still slightly damp. He wore an expensively styled suit that fitted perfectly across his broad shoulders and made him look incredibly masculine.

They went out to the car and he drove them along the coast road to the restaurant. He was unusually quiet on the journey, a bit subdued, and she wondered if something had happened at work to disturb him. Was it something to do with his sister? Or perhaps he was simply tired after a stressful day. She remembered feeling like that sometimes after a bad day at work.

It might not be a good idea to bombard him with questions right away, though. If he wanted to talk to her about whatever it was that was bothering him, he would be more likely to do it after he had relaxed into the evening a little.

He took her to a pretty quayside restaurant, and they sat at a table by the window, from where they could look out at the boats in the harbour.

'It's lovely in here,' she said, looking around. 'It's very peaceful and intimate.' There were screened alcoves with candlelit tables, a glass-fronted display cabinet showing mouth-watering desserts, and waiters who hovered discreetly in the background. 'It makes me want to skip the meal and go straight for the dessert,' she said, eying up the assortment of gateaux and fruit tarts.

He laughed. 'You always did go for the dessert.'

'Did I?' Her brow puckered. 'Have we done this before?'

He nodded cautiously. 'Don't worry about it,' he said. 'Just relax and enjoy the food.'

She tried to do as he suggested, but at the back of her mind she was trying to work out why, if they had been a couple at one time, they had drifted apart, with her working in Hampshire and Matt here in Devon. What wasn't he telling her?

Through the starter of freshly dressed crab served with asparagus spears and mayonnaise they talked about her starting work in a week's time, and then moved on to generalities, but Matt said nothing about what might be troubling him. They chatted and she could tell he was making an effort, being as considerate and thoughtful as ever.

He ordered a bottle of wine, and Saffi took a sip, studying him as the waiter brought the main course, sirloin of beef with red wine sauce. 'You're not yourself this evening,' she said softly, when they were alone once more. 'What's wrong?'

He blinked, and then frowned slightly. He wasn't eating, but instead he ran his finger around the base of his wine glass. 'I'm sorry. It's nothing. I'm just a bit preoccupied, that's all, but I didn't mean to spoil the evening.' He smiled at her. 'You were saying you were thinking of buying a new car?'

'Well, I'll need one if I'm going to start work. But that's not important right now. I want to know what's wrong, Matt. Something's troubling you. Is it your sister?'

He sighed heavily and then nodded. 'I've seen the results of the tests and the CT scan. They've diagnosed Zollinger-Ellison syndrome.'

She pulled in a quick breath. 'Oh, no…no wonder you're feeling down… I'm so sorry, Matt.' It was bad news. She laid her hand over his, trying to offer him comfort, and he gave her fingers an answering squeeze.

She really felt for him. Zollinger-Ellison syndrome was an illness caused by a tumour or tumours in the duodenum and sometimes in the pancreas, too. They secreted large amounts of the hormone gastrin, which caused large amounts of stomach acid to be produced, and in turn that led to the formation of ulcers. It was a very rare disease and there was around a fifty per cent chance that the tumours might be malignant. 'How is she? Does she know about it?'

'Yes, she knows. Obviously, it was a huge shock for her, but she was trying to put on a brave face for Ben.'

'Will they try surgery?'

He nodded. 'As a first stage of treatment, yes. The Whipple procedure would be the best option, but it's difficult and very specialised surgery, as you probably know. If the tumours have spread to other parts of her body they won't even consider it. We'll just have to take things one step at a time.'

'It's hard to take in. I've heard it might go better if

the patient has chemotherapy before surgery as well as afterwards.' She reflected on that for a while, knowing just how terrible it must be for Gemma and Matt to have to go through all this heartache.

She said, 'If there's anything I can do…does Gemma want any more books, or magazines, anything that will help to take her mind off things? I could perhaps find her some DVDs if she'd prefer?'

'Thanks, Saffi. I think she still has some of the magazines you sent last week. Maybe some comedy DVDs might help to take her mind off things for a while. Perhaps we can sort something out between us? I tried taking her fruit and chocolates but, of course, she has to be careful what she eats. Some things disagree with her.'

'We'll find something.'

They went on with their meal for a while, but somehow the pleasure in tasting the perfectly cooked meat and fresh vegetables had waned. She said quietly, 'Do your parents know?'

'Yes, I phoned my mother this afternoon. She was at work—she's a vet up in Cheltenham. She was so upset she said she was leaving everything and coming over right away.'

'I expect that will be good for Gemma.'

He nodded. 'My father's a GP in Somerset. He's going to try and get a locum to cover his practice for a while.'

'Your parents are divorced, then? I hadn't realised. Did that happen a long time ago?'

'When I was a child, yes.' His eyes were troubled. 'I was about eight years old when they broke up. Gemma

was younger. It was fairly traumatic for both of us…
though I suppose it often is for the children if it's a fairly
hostile split.'

He leaned back in his seat as the waiter came to clear
the dishes and take their order for dessert. He swallowed
some of his wine, and then refilled Saffi's glass.

'We chose to stay with my mother—Gemma and I.
My father could be distracted by work and we didn't always get to see much of him.' He pulled a face. 'Then
about three years later my mother had a sudden illness
that affected her kidneys and we were taken into foster-
care for a while.'

Saffi sucked in a breath. 'Is she all right now? It must
have been a double blow to go through the break-up of
your family and then to have that happen.' She frowned,
trying to imagine what it would have been like to endure
such an emotional upset.

'I think she's all right. While she was in hospital,
they managed to prevent the worst of the kidney damage, but she has to take medication now to control her
blood pressure and cholesterol, to make sure there aren't
any further problems. She sees a specialist once a year,
and things seem to be going well for her, as long as she
follows the dietary advice he's given her.' He was quiet
for a moment. 'I think she's the reason I wanted to study
medicine.'

The waiter brought dessert, a pear tatin with vanilla
ice cream, and Saffi ate, almost without knowing what
she was eating. 'I'd no idea you had such a troubled

childhood,' she said. 'But I suppose it was better for you once your mother was out of hospital?'

'Yes, it was.' He toyed with his food. 'Gemma and I had been in separate foster-homes for quite a long time, and that was tough. We were taken away from everything that made us feel safe.' He lifted his glance to her. 'But I don't suppose it was much worse than what you went through. After all, your parents died, didn't they?'

'They did, but I was quite young when that happened. And I had Aunt Annie. She stepped in right away and was like a mother to me. My uncle was there as well until two or three years ago, so he became a father figure for me.'

She dipped her spoon into the tart and savoured the taste of caramelised fruit on her tongue. 'Did you see much of your father back then?'

'Quite a bit. We'd spend time with him whenever he had a free weekend, but then he married again and his wife already had children of her own. We didn't get on all that well with them. We tried, of course, but they were older than me and Gemma and I think they resented us.'

'Oh, dear. That doesn't sound good. It must have been awkward for you.'

He smiled. 'Probably, as children, you take these things more or less in your stride. It's only when you get to adulthood and you look back that you realise it could have been a lot better, or maybe that you could have handled things differently. I was more or less okay with my father getting married again, but when my mother did the same thing I wasn't too happy.' He pulled a face. 'I was quite rebellious for a time.'

Saffi studied him thoughtfully as he signalled to the waiter and ordered two cappuccinos. 'Do you think it's had an effect on you?' she asked when the waiter left. 'Now, I mean, as an adult.'

He mused on that for a while. 'Possibly. I suppose it makes you cautious. But it's probably worse when you're an adolescent. Your emotions are all over the place anyway then. At one time I began to think I didn't really belong anywhere. I looked out for Gemma—that was the one thing that was constant.'

'Maybe that's why you can't settle into relationships now—the reason you bale out when things start to get serious—because deep down you think it could all go wrong and then it would be heart-wrenching for you all over again.'

He looked startled for a second or two, but he mused on that for a while, and then he frowned. 'I hadn't thought of it that way,' he said. He gave a crooked smile. 'I think you could be right. Men are supposed to be tough, but even they can have their hearts broken.'

She stirred brown sugar crystals into her coffee and stayed silent, deep in thought. *Once bitten?* Had some woman broken his heart in years past? Perhaps that had reinforced his conviction that he must steer clear of getting too deeply involved. Was it the reason he seemed to have so much trouble dealing with his feelings for her?

Maybe it might have been better if she'd never worked out the cause of his reluctance to commit long term. If he started going over past decisions in his mind, would he soon start to have second thoughts about seeing Gina again?

When they left the restaurant, it was still fairly early, and they walked along the quayside for a while, looking at the yachts in the harbour. He put his arm around her bare shoulders and said softly, 'I'm sorry for weighing you down with my problems. I wanted this to be a pleasant evening.'

'It was. It is. Perhaps we should do it again some time.' Her face flushed a little as she realised how pushy that sounded, and she added hurriedly, 'I mean, when you're not so troubled and you can relax a bit more.'

He smiled. 'I'd really like that.' They stopped by a railing and looked out over the bay in the distance, formed by tall cliffs and a long promontory. Waves lapped at the shore and splashed over the rocks. Further out, a lighthouse blinked a warning to any passing ships.

After a while, he checked his watch and said soberly, 'I suppose we should start heading for home. I wish we didn't have to break up the evening like this. I want to be with you...' He smiled wryly. 'I'm beginning to resent this Jason before I've even met him.'

He linked his fingers in hers as they started to walk back to the car. It felt good, just the two of them, hand in hand, and she, too, wished the evening didn't have to end.

It was still well before nine o'clock when they arrived home, but Saffi was dismayed to find that there was a black car parked on the drive. As she and Matt approached the house, the driver's door opened and a man stood up and came to greet them. He was tall, with crisply styled brown hair and hazel eyes. He wore a beautifully tailored dark suit.

'Saffi, it's so good to see you again.' Before she could guess his intention, Jason had put his arms around her and drawn her to him in a warm embrace. Beside her, she felt Matt stiffen.

Saffi froze. Jason was a virtual stranger to her and she had no idea how to react. She had the strong feeling he would have kissed her, too, but he seemed to gain control of himself just in time and released her. Maybe he realised she wasn't responding to him as he might have expected.

She felt bad about her reaction. 'I…uh…Jason…hello. I don't think you know Matt, do you? He lives in the annexe over there.' She waved a hand towards the end of the building. 'He's been really helpful to me, one way and another, these last few weeks.'

Jason frowned, and it seemed like an awkward moment, but Matt nodded a guarded acknowledgement of him and said, 'She's been through a bad time, so I've been looking out for her. I mean to go on doing that.'

Something in the way he said it made Saffi glance at Matt. Perhaps he'd meant it as a subtle warning, but Jason didn't seem put out.

She said, 'Thanks for coming over here, Jason. It was good of you to do that.'

'I was glad to. I wanted to see you again.'

'You came to see me in hospital, didn't you?'

He nodded. 'I'd have visited more often, but the nurses wouldn't let me. Then your flatmate kept sending me away, saying you weren't up to seeing people. Can you believe it—after all we meant to one another? I'm just so glad that we can finally be together.'

She heard Matt's sudden intake of breath and she made a shuddery gasp. It was no wonder he was alarmed by what Jason was saying. It had come as news to her, too.

Her cheeks flooded with sudden heat. How could she tell Jason that she didn't know him? He seemed to think things were exactly as they had been before—that they could go back to whatever relationship they'd had before she'd suffered her head injury.

'I...I'm still having trouble remembering things, Jason,' she said in a soft voice. 'I'm sorry, but I still don't know who you are and I don't think we can go back to how we were. It's not possible.'

Jason shook his head. 'I know it was a bad thing that happened to you, Saffi, but I'm not going to give up on what we had. Even if you've lost your memory, we can start again.'

Saffi looked at him, a feeling of apprehension starting up in her stomach. 'I don't think that's possible, Jason. Things are different now. I'm not the same person I was back then, back in Hampshire.'

'I don't believe that's true, Saffi. People don't change, deep down. And I won't give up on you. How can I? I won't rest until things are back to how they should be. You mean everything to me, Saffi. We love one another. We were practically engaged. It'll be the same again, you'll see.'

Saffi stared at him in disbelief. Engaged? Was it true? Matt was looking stunned by the revelation and she felt as though the blood was draining out of her. A feeling of dread enveloped her. How could she even consider being with another man when in her heart she knew she wanted Matt?

But wasn't that the worst betrayal of all, wanting to have nothing at all to do with a man she was supposed to have loved?

Distraught, she looked at Matt. She was shattered by everything Jason had said.

'Let's not get ahead of ourselves,' Matt said, his gaze narrowing on Jason. 'Whatever was between you two before this has to go on the back burner. She's in shock. She doesn't know you. You have no choice but to let it go for now.'

CHAPTER SEVEN

MATT HELPED JASON to unload the boot of his car, and between the three of them they carried Saffi's belongings into the house. The men seemed to have come to a mutual agreement that there would be no more talk of what had gone on in the past, and gradually Saffi felt the shock of Jason's announcement begin to fade away. Had they really been on the point of getting engaged?

After a while she managed to find her voice once more and she tried to make general conversation, wanting to ease the tension that had sprung up between the two men.

Neither of them said very much, but when they had finished the work, they both followed her into the kitchen. Matt was making no attempt to return to the annexe, and she suspected he had no intention of leaving her alone with Jason.

'My coffee-maker,' she said with a smile, unpacking one of the boxes. 'I've really missed it. Who's for espresso?'

She spooned freshly ground coffee into the filter and added water to the machine. It gave her something to do, and helped to take her mind off the awfulness of her situation. She'd been thoroughly shaken by events, so much so that her hands were trembling. Turning away, she tried to hide the tremors by going to the fridge and pouring milk into a jug.

Matt was frowning, his dark eyes watching Jason, assessing him. 'How long will you be staying in Devon?' he asked, and Saffi was grateful to him for taking over the conversation for a while. She felt awkward, out of her depth and she had no idea what to do about it.

'A couple of weeks,' Jason answered. 'I've booked into a hotel in town.'

Saffi handed him a cup of coffee. 'Chloe said you were taking some time off work…' She pulled a face. 'I don't even know what it is that you do.'

'I'm a medical rep. I generally work in the Hampshire area, and sometimes further afield if an opportunity crops up.'

'And you were working near to here today?'

'That's right, but I'd already made up my mind to come and see you. I just wanted to be near you, Saffi.' His gaze was intent, his hazel eyes troubled. 'We were so close before the accident. I want to be with you and make it like it was before. We can do that, can't we?'

She looked away momentarily, unable to face the yearning in his expression. He seemed to be in such an agony of emotion—how was it that she could have forgotten him, feel nothing for him, and yet apparently they had been so close? She was overwhelmed by guilt.

'I don't know what to say to you, Jason. I don't know

what to do.' She frowned, trying to work things out in her mind. Why did this have to happen…especially now, when she cared so much for Matt? But how could she simply turn Jason away? That would be heartless, like a betrayal of whatever relationship they'd once had. Was she the kind of person who could do that?

She said quietly, 'I know this must be very difficult for you. Perhaps we could get to know one another again…take it slowly…but I can't make any promises. I don't know how things will turn out. Things have changed. I'm not the same person any more.'

'What are you trying to say to me?' Jason's mouth made a flat line. 'Are you telling me you feel differently because you're with him?' He looked pointedly at Matt, a muscle in his jaw flicking.

She closed her eyes for a second or two, a tide of anxiety washing through her. 'Yes, I think I am.' She let out a long, slow breath. She'd said it. Admitted it. She'd known what the consequences might be when she couldn't stay away from Matt. She'd flirted with danger. Matt didn't want a long-term relationship, he had been clear on that, but she'd gone ahead anyway, getting herself in deeper and deeper.

Standing beside her, she saw Matt brace his shoulders. His lips were parted slightly as though on a soft sigh…of relief, or was he concerned now because she might want their relationship to be more serious? He didn't say anything, though, but looked fixedly at Jason.

Jason's mouth was rigid. 'You don't love her,' he said. 'You can't possibly care for her as I do. You've only known her for five minutes…how can that compare with what Saffi and I have shared?'

Matt pulled a wry face. 'Actually, you're wrong about that. I've known Saffi for years. The irony of it is that she doesn't remember me either.'

Jason looked stunned. After a second or two he recovered himself and said briskly, 'So, we're on an even footing. We'll see who comes out of this the winner, won't we?'

'True.'

Saffi stared at both of them, a wave of exasperation pulsing through her. 'Have you both finished discussing me as though I'm some kind of commodity to be shifted from one place to another as you please?' she enquired briskly. 'I think it's time for you both to leave.'

Stunned by her sharp rebuke, they did as she asked, albeit with great reluctance. Jason said goodbye, stroking her arm in a light caress, hesitant, as though he wanted to do more, perhaps to take her in his arms. Finally, he went to his car and drove off towards town.

Matt stood on the drive, watching him turn his car onto the country lane.

Saffi raised her brows questioningly. 'You're still here,' she said.

He gave her a wry smile. 'I'm just making sure you're safe,' he murmured, and then with a gleam in his eyes he added, 'If you begin to feel anxious in the night, or you want some company, you only have to bang on the wall and I'll be there in an instant.'

'Hmm…thanks for that, I appreciate it. But don't hold your breath, will you?' she murmured.

His mouth made an amused twist. 'You think I'm joking. Believe me, I'm not. Are you sure you don't want me to stay? After all, a few minutes ago you admitted you had feelings for me.' He moved closer as if to take her in his arms but she dragged up a last ounce of courage and put up a hand to ward him off.

'I can't do this, Matt,' she said huskily. 'I want to, but I can't. Not now. My whole life has been turned upside down and I don't know what to do or what to think. I need some space.'

He laid his hands lightly on her shoulders. 'I'm sorry. It's just that I hate to think of you being with that man—with any man. Seeing him with you has come as such a shock it's making me reassess everything.' He frowned. 'I don't mean to put pressure on you, Saffi, but you must know I want you…I need you to know that. I want you for myself. I want to protect you, to keep you from harm, in any way I can.'

'I'm not sure you would feel the same way if I hadn't lost my memory.' She shook her head. 'It makes a difference, doesn't it?'

'I don't know. All I know is I've always wanted you, Saffi. I've tried to fight against it, but I can't help myself. It seems like I've longed for you for ever and a day.'

Wanting wasn't the same as loving, though, was it? She daren't risk her happiness on a man who couldn't settle for one woman in his life. More and more she was growing to understand that it was what she wanted above all else—to have Matt's love and to know that it was forever.

'Things are all messed up,' she said softly. 'I don't know who I am or how to respond any more.'

Briefly, he held her close and pressed a gentle kiss to her forehead. 'Just follow your instincts,' he said, 'and know that I'm here for you, whenever you need me.'

He was still watching her as she went back into the house and closed the door. Alone once more, Saffi leaned back against the wall and felt the spirit drain out of her. Everything that she was, or had been, was locked up inside her head. Why didn't she know what had happened between her and Jason? Why had she and Matt parted company all those years ago? If only she could find the key to unlock the secrets hidden in her mind.

Jason came to call for her the next day, after Matt had left for work, and they spent time walking in the village and exploring the clifftop walks nearby. Perhaps he'd had time to think things through overnight, because he seemed to be doing everything in his power to help ease her mind. He made no demands of her, so that after a while she was able to relax a little with him. He told her about his job as a representative for a pharmaceutical company, and how it involved meetings with hospital clinicians, GPs and pharmacists.

In turn, she told him about her love for the house she'd inherited, the time she spent in the garden or looking after the hens and the beehives.

'I'll have to collect the honey soon,' she told him.

'You could help if you want. I could find you some pro-tective clothing.'

'I could never have imagined you doing such things,' he said with a grin. 'You were always so busy, working in A and E. You loved it. It was your passion.'

'Was it?' She couldn't be certain, but it felt as though he was right. 'I'll be doing it again in a few days' time.'

He frowned. 'You will? Are you sure you're up to it? How are you going to manage things at the house if you do that? The garden's huge. That's a full-time job in itself, without the hassle of looking after the hens.'

'It's not so bad. Matt helps with everything, espe-cially the bigger jobs around the place, like repairing fences or painting the hen coop. He's been keeping the lawns trim and so on. Besides, I'll only be working part time to begin with.'

'Even so, you don't need all this bother. You've been ill, Saffi. Why don't you sell up and come back to Hamp-shire? Life would be a lot easier for you there, and you would have friends around you.'

She shook her head. 'I don't remember anyone back there and I wasn't getting better. I was frightened all the while, and I didn't know why. It's different here. I love this house. It's my home, the place where I spent my childhood and where I felt safe.'

Jason wasn't happy about her decision, and she knew he wanted her to return to Hampshire with him, but he said no more about it. She saw him most days after that, while Matt was out at work, and he was always careful not to push things too far. Perhaps he was hoping her memory would return and they could take up where they had left off, but that didn't happen.

Although she knew Matt hated her being with Jason, he didn't try to persuade her against seeing him. Instead, he was there every evening, helping her with whatever needed to be done about the place. She discovered one of the hens, Mitzi, had a puncture wound in her leg and he cleaned it up while she gently held the bird to stop her from struggling.

'I think she might have broken the leg,' he said with a frown. 'I'll use some card as a splint and bind it up. Then we'll take her along to the vet.' He looked around. 'It's hard to see how she's managed to hurt herself—unless she was panicked in some way and fell against the timbers.'

'Perhaps we should keep her separate from the others for a while?'

He nodded. 'I'll sort out something for her. I think there's an old rabbit cage in the shed. I'll scrub it out and make it as good as new and it should make a good place for her to rest up.'

'Okay. Thanks.' She smoothed Mitzi's feathers. 'You'll be all right,' she said soothingly. 'We'll look after you.'

The vet prescribed antibiotics, a painkiller and splinted the leg properly. 'Keep her quiet for a few days, away from the other hens. She should heal up in a few weeks. Bring her back to me next week so that I can see if the leg's mending okay.'

'We will, thank you.' They went back to the house and settled her down in her new home.

'Maybe we could let her out on the grass on her own when she's feeling a bit more up to it?' Saffi suggested. She went over to the garden table and poured juice into a tumbler.

'Yes, we can do that. If it looks as though she's going to flap about too much, we'll pop her back in the cage.'

He sat down on one of the redwood chairs and she slid a glass towards him. He stared into space for a while, unseeing, and she guessed his thoughts were far away.

'Are you all right? Are you thinking about your sister? Have they operated on her? You said they were deciding on the best course of treatment.'

'That's right. They had to find out how far the disease had gone…whether it had spread beyond the pancreas and duodenum, but it seems she's in luck as far as that goes. They're bringing in a specialist surgeon to perform the Whipple procedure.'

She stood at the side of him and reached for his hand, wanting to comfort him as best she could. It was major surgery, a complicated procedure where part of the pancreas and the small intestine were removed, along with the gall bladder and part of the bile duct. After that had been done, the remaining organs would be reattached.

'When will they do it?'

'Next week. She's having a course of chemotherapy first to try and make sure it goes no further than it already has. They're going to do minimally invasive surgery, through laparoscopy, so there should be less chance of complications.'

Saffi bent down and put her arms around him. 'If you hadn't insisted on taking her to hospital, things could have been much worse. You've done everything you can for her, Matt.'

'Yeah.' He sighed. 'It just doesn't seem like nearly enough.'

'You're looking after Ben again, aren't you? Has his father gone back to work?'

He nodded. 'James is worried sick about Gemma and about the effect it's having on Ben. He was at the hospital all the time, but now he has to go away on an urgent callout. He's going to make sure he's back here when she has the surgery. I think this illness has really shaken him up.'

'I don't suppose Ben's reacting too well to all the changes going on in his life. Perhaps he can help me with the honey—not the collecting of it but afterwards, when I put it into jars?'

'I think he would enjoy that. When are you planning on doing it?'

'At the weekend.' She made a wry face. 'I thought I would open up the hives on Saturday, around lunchtime, when, like you said, most of the bees would be out and about.'

'Good idea. I'll give you a hand.'

She smiled at him. 'Thanks. I wasn't looking forward to doing it on my own for the first time.' Jason had said he had to be somewhere else on that particular morning, and she wondered if he had a problem with bees, or was worried about being stung. He still maintained she ought to sell up and leave everything behind.

Matt shot her a quick glance. 'How do you feel about going into work next week?'

Her mouth made a brief downward turn. 'I'm a bit apprehensive, to be honest. I'm worried that being able to help Josh might have been a once-only thing, and that I was working purely on instinct. I feel pretty sure I know what I'm doing, but I'd hate to come across something that I couldn't handle.'

'I don't think that's going to happen, because the way you were with Josh everything you did seemed skilful and automatic, as though it was part of you. And after talking to you the hospital chiefs are confident that you'll be fine. But if you're worried, you could come to the hospital with me tomorrow, just to observe and help out... if you want to. There's no pressure.'

'That's probably a good idea. I might get to know one way or the other if it's going to work out.'

'Okay. That's a date.' He grinned. 'Not the sort I'd prefer, but I guess it'll have to do for the time being.'

He picked her up in the morning after breakfast and drove her to the hospital. 'I'll introduce you to everyone, and after that you can just watch what's going on, or you can work alongside me,' he said as they walked into A and E. 'If you feel uncomfortable at any time, just let me know.'

She looked around. Everything seemed familiar to

her, and perhaps that was because she'd been here before with the little boy, Charlie, who had broken his leg and pelvis in the road accident. He was doing well now, by all accounts. She hadn't taken it all in then, but now she saw the familiar layout of an emergency unit.

'I think I'd like to work with you,' she said. 'If you'll show me where everything is kept.'

He put an arm around her shoulder and gave her a quick hug. 'Brilliant. I know you can do it, Saffi. It'll be as though you've never been away, you'll see.'

She wasn't so sure about that to begin with, but gradually, as the morning wore on, she gained in confidence, standing by his side as he examined his patients and talking to him about the problems that showed up on X-ray films and CT scans. It was a busy morning, and they finally managed to take a break several hours after they had started work.

'It's finally calmed down out there,' she said, sipping her coffee. 'It's been hectic.'

He nodded. 'You seem to be getting on well with Jake, our registrar, and the nurses on duty.'

'They've been really good to me, very helpful and kind.' Except that Gina Raines had come on duty a short time ago, and straight away Saffi had become tense. She wasn't sure why, but she had a bad feeling about her. Maybe it was because she knew she and Matt had been involved at one time, but that was over now, wasn't it? So why should that bother her now? As soon as she had seen her, though, a band of pain had clamped her head and her chest muscles had tightened.

She frowned. 'They all know about my head injury. I know we talked about telling them, but it feels odd.'

'I thought it best to be straight with everyone from the start, to explain what we're doing and why you're here. They're a good bunch of people. You'll be fine with them.'

'Yes. I think it will work out.' She took another sip of coffee and all of a sudden her pager went off. Matt checked his at the same time, and stood up, already heading towards the door. Saffi hurried after him.

'A five-year-old is coming in with her mother,' the triage nurse said. 'The little girl had just finished eating a biscuit at a friend's house when she felt dizzy and fainted. Now she can't get her breath.'

Matt and Saffi went to meet the mother in the ambulance bay, and quickly transferred the child to a trolley. It was clear to see that she was struggling to get air into her lungs, and a nurse started to give her oxygen through a mask.

'She's been saying her tummy hurts,' the distressed mother said, 'and she's been sick a couple of times in the car. She's getting a rash as well.'

They rushed her to the resuscitation room and the child's mother hurried alongside the trolley, talking to her daughter the whole time, trying to soothe her.

'Has Sarah had any problems with fainting before, or with similar symptoms?' Matt asked.

'She's never fainted, but she does have asthma, and she had a bit of a reaction to peanuts once.'

'Did she see her GP about the reaction?'

The woman shook her head. 'It was quite mild, so we didn't bother.'

'All right, thanks,' Matt said. 'You can stay with us in Resus. The nurse will look after you—if you have any questions, anything at all, just ask her.' He indicated Gina, who went to stand with the mother as they arrived in the resuscitation room.

It looked very much as though Sarah was having a reaction to something she'd eaten. Her face was swollen, along with her hands and feet. Saffi handed Matt an EpiPen, an automatic injector of adrenaline, and he smiled briefly, knowing she had intercepted his thoughts.

'Thanks.' He injected the little girl in the thigh, and Saffi handed him a syringe containing antihistamine, which he injected into the other leg. Then he began his examination, while a nurse worked quickly to connect the child to the monitors that gave readings of heart rate, blood pressure and blood oxygen. Everyone was worried about this little girl who was fighting for her life.

'Blood pressure's falling, heart rate rising. Blood oxygen is ninety per cent.'

'Okay, let's get a couple of lines in to bring her blood pressure up. I'll intubate her before the swelling in her throat gets any worse. And we need to get her legs up to improve her circulation—but be careful, we don't want to cause more breathing problems.'

After five minutes the child was still struggling with the anaphylactic shock. 'I'll give her another shot of adrenaline,' Matt said, 'along with a dose of steroid.'

The medication was already in Saffi's hand and she quickly passed it to him. They had to work fast. This was a life-threatening condition and they had to do everything they could to bring down the swelling and restore her life signs to a safe level.

Matt looked concerned, anxious for this small child, but he followed the treatment protocol to the letter.

'Her breathing's still compromised,' Saffi murmured. 'Should we give her nebulised salbutamol via the ventilator circuit?'

'Yes, go ahead. It should open up the air passages.'

A short while later they could finally relax and say that the child was out of immediate danger. They were all relieved, and Matt took time out to talk to the girl's mother and explain the awful reaction that the girl had experienced.

'We'll send her to a specialist who will do tests,' he said. 'We need to know what caused this to happen. In the meantime, we'll keep her here overnight and possibly a bit longer, to make sure that she's all right. We'll give you an EpiPen and show you how to use it so that you can inject Sarah yourself if anything like this happens again. You'll need to bring her straight to Emergency.'

He took the woman to his office so that he could talk to her a bit more and answer any of her questions.

Saffi went home later that day, satisfied that she had managed a successful day at work. She felt elated, thrilled that she was back on form, workwise at least.

Matt came to find her in the garden the next day when she was getting ready to open up the beehives. She'd brought out the protective clothing and laid it down on the table in preparation.

'Two new skills in one week,' he said with a smile. 'You're really up for a challenge, aren't you? You did really well yesterday. How did it feel to you, being back in a hospital?'

'It was so good,' she said, returning the smile. 'Like you said, it felt as though I'd never been away. I remembered everything about medicine, and how much I love being a doctor, the way Jason said I did.'

His brows drew together at the mention of Jason. 'How are you getting on with him?' he asked cautiously. 'Have you remembered how it was with you two before the accident?'

She shook her head. 'From time to time I get flashbacks, of places we've been, or brief moments we've shared, the same as I do with you and me, when we were once together, but they're so fleeting that I can't hold onto them.' Her glance met his. 'You still don't like him being here, do you?'

He winced. 'It shows? I thought I was doing a pretty good job of hiding it.' He moved his shoulders as though he was uncomfortable with the situation. 'Of course, he's been quite open about the fact that he wants you back, and I can scarcely blame him for that. You're a special kind of woman, and who wouldn't want to be with you? But I wish he'd stayed back in Hampshire.'

She studied him for a moment or two, frowning. 'It's more than that, isn't it? You really don't like him.'

'I think it's odd that he hasn't come to find you before this. I would have moved heaven and earth to find you if I was in his shoes.'

His brow furrowed. 'He's putting pressure on you—subtle pressure, but it's there all the same. He says you were practically engaged, but "practically" isn't the same as having a ring actually on your finger, is it? I can't help wondering if he's exaggerating.'

'Does that matter? Wouldn't you do the same if you really cared about someone?'

'I do care about someone—I care very deeply for *you*, Saffi. I've never felt this way before—you can't imagine how badly it hurts to see you with someone else.'

She pressed her lips together. She didn't want to hurt him. It grieved her to see the pain in his eyes, but she was torn. She loved Matt, deeply, intensely, but didn't she owe Jason something, too?

To turn her back on him would be a betrayal. He would feel she hadn't even given him a chance. She didn't want to hurt anyone, but she desperately wanted Matt.

She lifted her arms to him, running her palms lightly over his chest. 'Isn't that a kind of pressure you're using, too? I don't want to see you hurting, Matt. That's the last thing I want.'

He gave a ragged sigh, the last of his willpower disintegrating as her hands trailed a path over his chest and moved up to caress the line from his neck to his shoulders.

He pulled her to him and kissed her fiercely, all his pent-up desire burning in that passionate embrace. His hands smoothed over her, tracing every feminine curve, filling her with aching need.

She clung to him, her fingers tangling in the silk of his hair, loving the way his body merged with hers, the way his strong thighs moved against her, and longing for him to say to her the one thing she wanted to hear.

She wanted his love, needed it more than anything in the world, but would it ever be hers?

'Saffi, I'm lost without you... What am I to do?' His voice was rough around the edges and she could feel his heart thundering in his chest.

The sun beat down on them and she felt heady with longing, fever running through her as his hand cupped her breast and his thumb gently stroked the burgeoning nub. A quivery sigh escaped her, and she looked up at him, her gaze meshing with his. More than anything, she wanted to give in to her deepest desires, to have him make love to her without any thought for the consequences.

But she couldn't do that. Not until she knew the truth about her past, about what had happened to spoil their relationship and send her headlong into Jason's arms.

Slowly, she came down to earth, and began to gently ease herself away from him.

Even as she did so, a small voice called in the distance, 'Uncle Matt, I finished my picture. Come and see.'

Matt gave a soft groan, releasing her and gazing at her with smoke-dark eyes full of regret.

'We have to sort out this thing with Jason,' he said huskily. 'I'm not going to share you with any man, in body or in spirit.'

CHAPTER EIGHT

'Hey, you've been out and bought yourself a new car!' Matt looked admiringly at Saffi's gleaming silver MPV. 'It looks great, doesn't it?'

'I'm pleased with it,' Saffi said, glad that he liked her choice. 'I need one so that I can get to and from work, so I went ahead and took the plunge yesterday.'

'I wonder how I managed to miss that? You must have put it straight in the garage while I was busy with something else.'

'Yes, I did. I was a bit overwhelmed by the time I arrived home—getting back behind the wheel and so on.'

Frowning, he put an arm around her. 'I would have gone with you if you'd said. Did you have any problems finding what you wanted?'

She shook her head. 'Actually, Jason went with me to the showroom.'

She felt Matt stiffen, and added hastily, 'I didn't have much choice in the matter. He came to see me and insisted on going along with me.'

'How can he insist on anything? He's not your keeper.'

She winced. 'True. But I feel so guilty about forgetting him… I'm finding it hard to make him understand that I need some space.'

'He's playing on your emotions.'

'Maybe. Anyway, he wasn't too happy with my choice of car. He thought I should have gone for something smaller, but I like the flexibility of this one. You can fold down the seats to create more storage space. That might come in useful if I ever have to carry medical equipment around with me.'

He smiled. 'Do you think you might want to try your hand at being an immediate care doctor?'

She chuckled. 'Perhaps I'd better not try to run before I can walk. But you never know.'

'Hmm.' He sobered. 'How does it feel to drive? I mean, you said you were a bit worried about it.'

'It's okay, I think. I didn't actually have a problem bringing it home, anyway.'

'That's good. One more hurdle out of the way.'

'Let's hope so. I thought I could drive us to the vet's with Mitzi after work today, if that's all right with you? Unless you'd like me to go on my own?'

'No, I'll go with you. I want to hear what the vet has to say. It's good to see other professionals at work, and it's useful to get their advice. You never know when it might come in handy. Besides, I like spending time with you. You know I do.' He frowned. 'I'd do it a lot more if it wasn't for Jason hanging around.'

He turned to go back into the house to get ready for work. 'I'll see you at the hospital in two ticks.'

'Okay.' She set off for the hospital, still smiling at

what he'd said. He liked spending time with her. It made her feel warm inside.

They met up in A and E a short time later, and even though this was her first official day at work, everything went smoothly. She treated a child who had come in with a broken collarbone after playing football at school and a girl who had dislocated her shoulder in a fall. There was also a tricky diagnosis where a boy had fallen and felt disorientated...it turned out to be a case of epilepsy.

Matt left her to get on with things pretty much on her own, but she was aware he was keeping an eye on her all the while. He needn't have worried, though, because she was absolutely sure of what she was doing, and after a while the whole team relaxed and treated her as one of themselves, as if she'd been there for years.

At lunchtime Matt disappeared, and she guessed he'd gone to check up on Gemma. She was having her surgery today, and although Matt had been as calm and as efficient as ever as he went about his work, she knew that he was worried about her.

When he returned to A and E after about half an hour, he said quietly, 'Shall we go and get a coffee?'

'That would be good. I'm ready for one.' She walked with him to the staffroom. 'How is Gemma?'

'She's still in Theatre, but everything's going well so far. Her vital signs are okay, which is good.' He fetched two coffees and they went to sit down. 'James is in the waiting room. He's in bad shape. He's terrified something might go wrong.'

'Whatever happened to break them up, it seems as though he really cares about her.'

He nodded. 'I think he does. I'm fairly sure it's his job that's the trouble, because he's away from home so often.'

'Can't he get some other kind of work?'

'That would be the best answer, and I think he realises it now. He says he's applying for posts close to home. His qualifications are good, so he shouldn't have too much trouble finding something suitable.'

She sipped her coffee. 'It's been a scary time for both of you.'

'Yeah.'

'Even so, I envy you, having a family, having someone close. I sometimes wish I'd had a brother or a sister. My aunt wasn't able to have children, so there weren't even any cousins.'

He looked at her, his eyes widening a fraction. 'Is that a new memory?'

'Oh!' She gave a laugh. 'Yes, it was. Perhaps you were right about me coming back to work. It must be opening up new memory pathways.'

They went back to A and E a few minutes later, and Saffi became engrossed once more in treating her patients.

She left for home a few hours before Matt, and spent the afternoon getting on with chores. Jason had wanted to meet up with her, but she'd put him off as she needed to make a trip to the grocery store.

'I could go with you,' he'd said. 'I just want to be with you.'

'I know, Jason, but I'd sooner do this on my own. Anyway, I'm going to the hairdresser and then to the vet's surgery later.' She didn't want to be with him for too long. She'd much rather be with Matt, and she suspected Jason knew that.

After Matt arrived home, she gave him time to grab a bite to eat and then she put Mitzi into a carrier ready for the journey to see the vet.

'Is there any news of Gemma?' she asked as they went over to her car. She slid into the driver's seat and Matt climbed in beside her.

'Well, she's out of surgery and in Intensive Care. Her blood pressure's very low and she's had several bouts of arrhythmia—they're obviously concerned. She's in a lot of pain, too, so they're giving her strong drugs.'

'At least she came through it, Matt.' She laid her hand on his arm. 'She's young, and that's in her favour.'

'Yeah, there is that.' He breathed deeply. 'And James is at her bedside. If she wakes up, she'll see him right away.'

She started the engine. 'Where's Ben today?'

'He's with my mother. She's staying at Gemma's house so that he's in familiar surroundings.'

'That's good. This is bound to be upsetting for him.'

A few minutes later she turned onto the tree-lined road where the vet's surgery was situated. They didn't have to wait long before they were called into his room and he examined Mitzi's leg once more.

'That seems to be healing up nicely,' he said. 'Sometimes the leg becomes crooked, but it looks as though she's doing really well. I'll give you some more antibiotics for the wound, and a few painkillers, although I think she probably won't need them for too long.'

Mitzi's ordeal was over in a few minutes and they put her in the carrier once more then went back to the car.

Saffi drove back to the village. There was a fair amount of traffic on the main road at this time of the evening, and she checked her rear-view mirror regularly along the way.

After a while, she noticed that a black car was edging into view, coming close up behind her. She frowned. Whoever was driving it had been following her for some time, getting nearer and nearer, and now she was beginning to feel uneasy. Because of the shadows she couldn't see the driver's face clearly, but seeing that car had sparked something in the darker regions of her mind. She was sure something like this had happened to her before, that she'd been followed along a busy road.

She indicated to turn off the main road, and breathed a soft sigh of relief as the black car made no signal to do the same. It had all been in her imagination. The car wasn't following her. It was going straight on.

She drove onto the country lane, and after a while she glanced into her rear-view mirror once more. The car was there again, right behind her. She gripped the steering-wheel tightly. Her heart was thudding heavily.

'Saffi, what's wrong?' Matt's voice sounded urgent. 'You're as white as a sheet.'

'I'm not sure,' she managed, 'but I think I'm being followed.' She pulled in a shaky breath. 'It's probably nothing. It's just that…'

She broke off, switching on her indicator and carefully bringing the car to a halt in a lay-by. Beads of sweat had broken out on her brow.

She looked in the mirror once more. The black car had slowed down, too, as though the driver was unsure of himself, but then at the last moment he pulled away and went on down the country lane.

Saffi leaned back in her seat and let the fear drain out of her. The image of that black car was imprinted on her mind.

'Can you tell me what happened?'

'I don't know. Perhaps I made a mistake.'

'You were frightened, Saffi. What was it that scared you? Is it because you were in a collision once before? Did it happen because someone was following you?'

She swallowed hard. 'I think so. I can't remember clearly. It was a dark-coloured car. Something happened…I think I was rammed from behind…then a man stepped out of the car and came over to me.' She searched her mind for anything more, but the image faded and she couldn't bring it back. 'All I know is I was terrified.'

He undid his seat belt and leaned towards her, wrapping his arms around her. 'No wonder you were scared. It would be a bad experience for anyone.' He stroked her hair. 'Did you report it to the police?'

She frowned. 'I don't think so. I don't know what happened after he came over to me.'

They sat for a while with Matt holding her until her heart stopped thumping and she felt as though she could go on.

'Would you like me to drive the rest of the way?'

She shook her head. 'No, thanks. I'll do it. I'll be all right now.' She wanted to stay in his arms, but at the same time she needed to overcome her fears. Slowly, she eased away from him.

He frowned. 'Okay…if you're sure.' He fastened his seat belt once more and she started the car, driving cautiously until they arrived home.

'If you want me to be a passenger in the car over the next few weeks until you're over this, that's fine by me,' Matt said after she'd settled Mitzi back in her cage.

'Thanks.' She smiled at him. 'I think I'll be okay.'

Somehow knowing what it was that had caused her worries about driving was enough to ease her mind. Whatever had happened was in the past and not something that she need be concerned about now. It was like a weight off her mind, and it meant that when she drove to work the next day she was calm and the journey was uneventful.

'You seem to have settled in here well,' Gina said, as she assisted her with a young patient who needed sutures in a leg wound. 'Are you getting to know your way around?'

'I think so,' Saffi answered. 'Everyone's been very helpful.'

'Yes, I found that, too.'

'Ah, of course—you came here just a few days before I started, didn't you?' She glanced at Gina, who was wearing her brown hair loose this morning, so that it fell in soft waves to the nape of her neck. 'You're covering for a maternity leave? What will you do when that contract finishes?'

'I'll go back to the community hospital. They let me do this as a way of gaining experience in other departments. The nursing chief is good like that. She thinks variety will make for better nursing, so she was willing to allow the transfer.'

'She's probably right.'

Saffi tied off the last suture and gave her small patient a smiley-face badge. 'You were very brave,' she said.

Gina stayed behind to clear the trolley while Saffi went off to examine a six-year-old who had breathing difficulties and a barking cough. The nurse seemed friendly, and she hadn't anticipated that. She'd wondered if there might be some tension between them since Gina had dated Matt, but working with her had been much easier than she'd expected.

Matt had gone to see his sister before coming into A and E this morning, and Saffi busied herself going about her work. Whenever she had a brief free moment she thought about the dilemma she was in, and what she should do about Jason. He'd been easygoing, good company, and she could perhaps see some small reason why they might have been a couple before the accident that had blighted her life.

She didn't have any feelings for him, though, and she was fairly certain that even if she were to spend several more weeks in his company she still wouldn't feel anything for him. Was that because something inside her had changed after her head injury, or was it because she had fallen in love with Matt?

What could she say to him? He would be going back to Hampshire in less than a week and he was begging her to go with him.

And what should she do about Matt? Emotionally, she was totally bound up in him. He wanted her and they were good together, but there was no future in the relationship that she could see. Wasn't she inviting heartache?

Matt walked briskly into A and E, breaking into her thoughts, and quickly glanced through the list of patients who were being treated. 'Any problems so far?' he asked, and the registrar shook his head.

'It's all under control.'

Saffi glanced at Matt, trying to gauge his mood. His expression was serious, and she wondered if everything was all right with his sister.

'How is she?' she asked.

His mouth flattened. 'She's feeling pretty awful at the moment. There are all sorts of tubes that have to be left in place for a while, as you know, and one of the insertion points is infected. They've taken swabs to find out what bacteria are involved, and put her on strong antibiotic cover in the meantime.'

'I'm sorry.'

The triage nurse cut across everyone's conversation just then, saying, 'Red alert, people. We've a child coming in by ambulance. Suspected head injury after a fall on a path at home. Estimated arrival ten minutes.'

Everyone was immediately vigilant, ready to do their designated jobs.

When the boy, Danny, was brought into the resuscitation room, Saffi's heart lurched. He was about the same age as Ben, and he looked so small and vulnerable, white-faced, his black hair stark against the pillows.

'He's been vomiting on the way here,' the paramedic said, but by now the child had slipped into unconsciousness.

Immediately, Matt began his assessment, while Saffi quickly set up a couple of intravenous fluid lines. A nurse connected Danny to monitors and Matt began a thorough examination of his small patient.

Once his vital signs had stabilised and Matt was satisfied there were no other major injuries, he said, 'Okay, let's get him over to Radiology for a CT head scan.'

Matt and Saffi went with the child. She was apprehensive, dreading what the scan might reveal. Head injuries like this were always serious and could be life-threatening. Danny's parents must be frantic with worry.

Seeing the results of the scan on the computer screen, Matt's jaw tightened. Saffi was filled with anxiety.

'Call Theatre,' Matt told Gina, who was assisting. 'Tell them I'm on my way with a four-year-old who has a subdural haematoma.'

'Are you doing the surgery?' Gina asked.

He nodded. 'There's no one else available right now. Prep the child and I'll go and scrub in as soon as I've spoken to the parents.' He looked at Saffi. 'Do you want to come and scrub in as well?'

'Yes. I'd like to.'

Everything happened very quickly after that. He explained to the parents that blood was leaking into the tissues around their child's brain and because it had no way of escaping it was building up dangerous pressure inside Danny's head. Left untreated, it could cause brain damage.

To prevent that, Matt had to make a hole in the boy's skull in order to release that pressure and remove any blood clots that had formed.

The boy's parents were stunned, and obviously terrified about what was happening to their child, but they signed the consent form and soon Danny was on his way to Theatre.

As soon as Danny had been anaesthetised, Matt worked quickly and carefully, aided by computer monitoring, to make a burr-hole in the child's skull. Saffi suctioned the wound to remove a huge clot that had formed, and then Matt controlled the bleeding with cauterisation and finished the procedure, inserting a drainage tube into the operation site.

Danny was still in danger, as Saffi knew only too well from her own experience of head injury, but at least he could be treated with drugs now to keep him sedated and bring down the swelling on the brain. The worry was whether he would have suffered any brain damage, but that might not become clear for some time.

Afterwards, Danny was taken to the recovery room where he was to be cared for by a specialist nursing team. Matt supervised the transfer. 'We'll send him over to Intensive Care just as soon as they're ready to receive him.'

He and Saffi started back down to A and E, and Matt said quietly, 'Are you due to go off home now? It must be about time for your shift to end.'

'Yes, it is. Why? Do you want me to stay for a bit longer?'

'I wondered if you have time for a coffee in my office. I need to record my case notes, but we could talk for a while.'

'Okay.' She followed him into the office and watched as he set up the coffee-machine in a small alcove.

He passed her a cup a few minutes later, and she stood with him, sipping the hot drink and admiring his strong, wonderfully capable hands and his long, powerful body as he leaned back against the worktop. They talked for a while, about his sister, their work, and the way her memory was coming back in fits and starts.

He put his arm around her, and she looked up at him.

'I'm glad I came to work with you,' she murmured. 'You're very good at what you do. Everyone here respects you and would do anything for you. And you were so efficient, so quick at getting Danny up to Theatre and then operating on him.'

'Sometimes you have to work fast.'

She nodded. 'I thought you were brilliant.'

He pretended to swagger. 'Well, I do my best.'

She smiled up at him, settling into his embrace, gazing at him in love and wonder. 'I mean it. You're a good teacher, too…I've watched you show junior doctors how to carry out difficult procedures. You're very patient.'

'You do realise this is all going to my head, don't you? I shall be too big for my boots at this rate.' He gave that some consideration. 'Hmm. Perhaps I'd better stop you from saying any more.' He drew her towards him and bent his head, capturing her lips with his own.

His kiss was gentle at first, exploring the sweetness of her mouth with such tenderness that it seemed he was brushing her lips with fire. Her body tingled with exhilaration. And all the time he was coaxing her to move in closer, his hand smoothing over the base of her spine and urging her against him. 'You're everything I want in a woman, Saffi,' he said in a roughened voice. 'I don't think you know what you do to me.'

'What do I do to you?' she asked mischievously, revelling in the way her soft curves were crushed against his hard body.

'Ahh…' he groaned, as though he was in pain. 'You know exactly what it is.' His dark gaze moved over her, and the breath snagged in his throat. 'I need you, Saffi. It makes my heart ache to think of you with another man.'

'I'm not with another man.'

'You are. You know who I mean…Jason.' He sucked in a shuddery breath. 'Will you be seeing him this afternoon?'

'Oh.' She gave a small sigh. 'Yes. He said he wanted to take me to a place along the coast.'

His eyes closed briefly as though he was trying to shut out the picture that formed in his mind. 'Promise me you won't fall for him, Saffi.'

'I'm not dating him, Matt. I'm just trying to help him…it must have been such a shock for him, knowing he was like a stranger to me. I thought, if we got to know one another, he might realise we have nothing.'

'Things don't quite work out like that, though, do they…the way we expect? You might suddenly remember what it was you had before.'

'Matt…'

He kissed her again, quelling the words before she could get them out, and her mind spun in a heady vortex of desire and longing, and all the while mixed up with it was a spiralling fear that uneasy suspicions might tear them apart.

She loved him. How could she ever leave him for another man? But, on the other hand, would he eventually tire of her and leave her for someone else? Someone like—

The image of a dark-haired temptress with sultry green eyes swam into her vision. In her mind, the girl was standing in a bedroom doorway, one hand resting on the doorjamb. She was dishevelled, her shirt falling open to show her bra and a skirt that was unbuttoned at the waist. Saffi recoiled as though she'd received a blow to the stomach. 'No…oh, no…'

'Saffi?' Matt looked at her in consternation. 'What

is it? Has something happened?' He stared at her, trying to work out what was going through her mind. 'Is it
another memory?'

'I...she...yes...she was there...she was with you...'
She broke away from him, aghast at the images that had
swirled through her mind.

The colour drained from Matt's face. 'Saffi, it's not
what you think. You have to believe me.'

She shook her head, as though that would shake off
the picture that was splashed across her vision like the
pages of a magazine.

She stared at him, shocked to the core. 'You know
what I'm seeing, don't you?' His words were like an
admission of guilt, even though he was denying it. 'No
wonder you wouldn't tell me what had happened between us.'

He moved towards her, reaching out to hold her, but
she backed away.

'You...you ch-cheated on me... Oh, no...'

She felt sick, her stomach was churning, her chest
heaving. The image, once forgotten, was now burned
on her mind.

'How could you? We were in love and you cheated
on me with Gina.'

Matt looked agonised. 'I tried to explain, but you
wouldn't listen. I didn't cheat on you, Saffi. I know it
must have looked that way, but I didn't.'

'She told me...she said you wanted her...that it was
all over between you and me. How can I believe you
when she told me herself what was going on?' She turned

away from him and rushed to the door. 'I have to get out of here.'

She heard him calling after her, but she ignored him and kept on going, out of the door, desperate to get away. The department's emergency phone began to ring, and as she stepped into the main area of the emergency unit she heard Matt's pager bleep. She knew he couldn't come after her now, and she fled to the car park, thankful that she had been able to make her escape.

CHAPTER NINE

'YOU'RE VERY QUIET today. Has something happened between you and Matt?'

Jason watched Saffi keenly, but she tried to avoid his gaze. They were sitting on the grass in a picnic area high up on the moor, overlooking a magnificent bay. 'I noticed that you keep trying to avoid him by going into the house whenever he's around in the garden. You did that yesterday and again this morning.'

'I'd rather not talk about it,' she said. 'Could we finish up here and go back to the house, do you think?' She hadn't wanted to come out at all this afternoon, but he'd persuaded her to come with him on a picnic and now she was regretting it. Her heart simply wasn't in it. She needed to be on her own, to think things through.

'But it's beautiful out here, don't you agree? It might help you to relax if we stay for a little longer. I picked this spot especially…it's peaceful and shaded from the sun, and we can see over the moor for miles.'

'I know. I'm sorry.' It was true that this was a lovely place to spend an afternoon, and for the most part she'd appreciated the peaceful riverside walk. They'd followed the path through the woods and come to this idyllic place, where they could sit and look at the coastline in the distance.

But she didn't want to be here with Jason. She wanted to be with Matt, but every time she thought about him her stomach turned over and she felt panicky and sick inside. How could he have let her fall in love with him all over again only to have the beautiful bubble of illusion burst in her face?

'Have some food,' Jason suggested, rummaging in the hamper and bringing out a pack of sandwiches. 'You've hardly eaten anything.'

'No, I'm not hungry. Thanks all the same.'

He held up a plastic container. 'How about a jellied fruit pot?'

'No, really. Thanks. You thought of everything, the food was excellent and this place is perfect, but I want to start back now.' Her head was hurting as the blood pounded through her veins and her forehead was hot.

He frowned. 'But I thought we could—'

She started to pack away the paper plates and packaging. 'Stay here, if you like,' she said, unable to cope any longer with his prevarication, 'but I'm going home.'

'Ah, come on, Saffi, don't be like that. I thought we might stay here for a bit and then wander down to the inn later on. We could head down that way now, if you want.'

She stood up. 'You're not listening to me, Jason. We've already been out for a few hours, when I didn't want to come here at all. It's my fault, I should never have agreed. But now I'm going home.'

She started to walk across the moorland, taking a short cut to where they'd left the car. Jason caught up with her and fell into step beside her.

'You've fallen out with him, haven't you?' he guessed, and when she didn't answer he said with quiet satisfaction, 'Well, I can't say I'm sorry. I'm glad he's out of the picture.' He gazed at her, his eyes filled with longing. 'You and I belong together, Saffi. I knew we were right for each other the moment we met.'

'I don't know about that,' she said. 'I still don't remember how it was before I hurt my head.'

He smiled. 'Perhaps if I kissed you, it would all come flooding back.'

A faint tremor ran through her. 'No,' she said, perhaps a little too firmly. 'That's not a good idea.'

He was quiet after that, walking along with her to the car, making desultory conversation.

It was a huge relief finally to be back at the house and when he asked if he could come in, she said softly, 'I want to be alone for a while, Jason. I think I'll go and lie down for a bit.'

She had a sick headache, and perhaps it was a result of the strain of these last few days, or maybe it was because everything was coming unglued inside her head and her memories were returning thick and fast. She'd longed for that to happen these last few months, but now she wished she could go back to her state of blissful ignorance.

At work in A and E it took a real effort not to let her unhappiness show. She spoke to Matt about their patients or anything medical, but whenever he tried to talk about what had happened between them she cut him off.

'I don't want to hear it, Matt,' she said in a fractured voice. 'We've been through this before. It's over.' Even though she'd managed to say it, inside she was falling apart. His expression was tortured, and she guessed he was full of regret for the way things had ended all over again. Her stomach churned to see the pain in his features, but it was all of his own doing, wasn't it? She couldn't be with a man who had cheated on her. Wasn't there always the chance he might do it again? Hadn't his love for her been strong enough to overcome temptation?

She finished her shift at the hospital and hoped Jason would stay away from her. She hadn't exactly been good to him the day before. But he turned up again a couple of hours after she returned home, full of plans for where they might go.

'We could drive over to Rosemoor and look around the garden,' he suggested. 'You'd love it there. There's an arboretum and a cottage garden—all the things you like.'

She shook her head. 'Not today, Jason. I think I'll just stay here and potter in the garden. There's quite a lot of tidying up to do.' She could see he was disappointed and she added gently, 'I know this is your holiday and you want to be with me, but I'm not in the best of moods. Perhaps you'd do better to look up old friends or go out and about by yourself.'

'No. I'll stay with you,' he said, and her heart sank. Sooner or later, she would have to tell him it would never work out for them. Perhaps she'd seen something in him at one time and they'd been good together, but, whatever it was, it had gone. It had taken her less than a fortnight to discover that they weren't suited.

She doubted she'd ever find love again. Matt had ruined her for that. For her, he was the one and only, but it looked as though he hadn't felt the same way about her. What had gone on between him and Gina was in the past, of course, but it could well happen again when he tired of her and she couldn't handle that.

Jason sat on the rustic bench and watched her as she carried out everyday gardening tasks, dead-heading flowers and pulling up the occasional weed. They talked as she worked, and he told her more about his job as a rep, and how they'd met up when he'd come to the hospital pharmacy back in Hampshire as she had been fetching medication for a patient.

She'd started to gather seed pods from the aquilegia when Ben wandered into the garden. 'Hi,' he said, giving her a big smile. 'What are you doing?'

'I'm collecting these pods from the flowers,' she said, showing him. 'They're full of seeds, see?' She shook some out into a small bowl. 'I'll put them into envelopes so that they can dry out, and then next year I can plant them in the ground. They'll grow into flowers.'

'Can I have some? When Mummy comes home, we can put them in the garden.'

'That's a good idea. I'll give some to your Uncle Matt to keep for you.' She didn't want him deciding to see what they tasted like. 'How is your mother? Have you been to see her?'

He nodded vigorously. 'We're going in a little while—me and Uncle Matt. She's feeling a bit better. She was sitting in a chair when we went to see her yesterday.' His eyes shone with excitement. 'My daddy's coming back home to live with us.'

'That's great, Ben.' She gave him a hug. 'I'm so pleased for you.'

Jason cleared his throat noisily, drawing her attention away from Ben, and when she turned towards him he said, 'All this talk about planting seeds—surely you're not thinking of staying here?'

She frowned. 'Yes, of course. I thought you realised that's what I wanted to do. I wasn't sure what I was going to do when I first came back here, but now I know it's what I want more than anything.'

'But I thought you would go back with me to Hampshire. You know that's what I want. We talked about it.'

She stared at him, aghast. How could he have assumed so much? She searched her mind for anything she might have said that could have given him the idea she had agreed to his suggestion, and came up with nothing.

'I'm not leaving here,' she said.

Ben tugged on her jeans. 'Can we go and look for some eggs?'

'Yes, okay.' She glanced at Jason and saw that he was scowling at the boy. He obviously didn't like the interruption.

'Jason,' she murmured, 'it looks as though I'm going to be spending some time with Ben now, and then I plan to have a quiet evening. Like I said, I'm not the best company today. Perhaps it would be best if you went back to your hotel.'

'We haven't had much time together,' he complained, 'with you working, and people dropping by.'

'People?' she echoed.

'All these distant neighbours that come by for flowers or vegetables—it wouldn't be so bad if they took the stuff and went away, but they stay and chat. And now the boy's come along to take up your time.'

Ben looked confused, sensing that something was wrong. Saffi put a comforting arm around the child and said, 'I like chatting with my neighbours, and I want Ben to feel that he can come round here whenever he wants.'

She hesitated, bracing herself for what had to be said. 'I think you should go, Jason. This isn't going to work out the way you hoped. I don't know how it was before, but I can't care for you the way you want. We're just not suited.'

'You feel that way because you've been ill, you suffered a bad head injury and it's taking time for you to get things back together again. We'll be fine. Give it time, Saffi.'

She shook her head. 'I'm sorry, Jason. I don't mean to hurt you, but you're so keen to see things the way they were that you're not giving any thought to the way I am now and what I feel and think.'

'We could work it out. You just have to give it time.'

He couldn't accept what she was telling him, and he countered everything she put to him with an argument of his own.

In the end, she said sadly, 'I can't do this any more, Jason. Please, go.'

Ben tugged once more at her jeans and she nodded, looking down at him. 'Yes, we'll go and see the hens.'

Jason left in a huff, and Saffi winced. Could she have been a bit more tactful or given him more time? Maybe, from his point of view, he had good reason to feel put out.

She went with Ben to the hen house and helped him to collect the eggs from the nesting boxes. 'Shall we see if Mitzi's left any for us?'

He nodded and they went over to the rabbit hutch. Matt had attached a wire run to the cage so that she could stretch her legs, and Ben was gleeful when he found two large brown eggs nestling in the wood shavings.

Matt came over to them as they started back towards the house. 'You've been busy,' he said, looking at the basket.

'We found six!' Ben said gleefully. 'They're for tea.' He thought about it. 'I could eat them all.'

Matt chuckled. 'You must be hungry. Do you think you could take them into the kitchen? Be careful.'

'I will.' Ben went off, holding the basket very still so as not to disturb the eggs.

Matt looked at Saffi, searching her face for some clue as to how she was feeling. 'How are you?' he asked.

She shrugged. 'I'm okay.'

He grimaced. 'I'd have done anything not to upset you.'

'Then perhaps you should have told me what happened before I started to care for you all over again,' she said sharply. 'You should have thought about it in the first place before you decided to two-time me with Gina. Or perhaps you imagined I wouldn't find out?'

His face was contorted with grief and regret. 'It didn't happen, Saffi—it wasn't what you thought.'

'Wasn't it?' Her eyes widened in disbelief. 'It seemed pretty straightforward to me. I dropped by your place one night when you weren't expecting to see me, and Gina came out of the bedroom. What am I supposed to make of it?'

'She was trying to get back with me. When you came by after your shift finished she took advantage of the situation and made it seem as if we'd been together.'

She was scornful. 'You've had a long time to think that one up, haven't you? There's no future for us, Matt. I told you at the time, I believe what I saw, and what she said. She told me you were getting back together. Why would I think differently?'

'Because you know me, and I'm telling you that's how it was.' His eyes darkened with sorrow. 'Or perhaps I'm wrong about that, and you never really knew me at all.'

'Obviously you're right about that.' There was pain in her eyes as she flung his words back at him. 'I thought I knew you, but you deceived me and I was devastated— twice over. I don't know how you could do that to me.' Her mouth tightened. 'And why *didn't* you tell me what had happened between us when we met up again instead of letting me find out weeks later?'

His brows shot up. 'Are you kidding? If I'd done that

I would never have had the chance to show you who I really am all over again. You wouldn't have had anything to do with me.' His mouth flattened. 'You can't imagine how difficult it's been for me to stay silent, or how hard it was for me to watch and wait for your memory to return, knowing all the while that you might cut me out of your life all over again.'

'You were right,' she said stiffly. 'That's exactly what I'd do. I couldn't be with anyone who played around.'

'I told you I didn't do that. I tried to explain, but you wouldn't listen and instead you left within the week and started a new life in Hampshire.' His grey eyes were bleak. 'You wouldn't take my calls, you wouldn't see me when I went over there—you wouldn't even speak to me at your aunt's funeral. Where does trust come into all this, Saffi?' There was an edge of bitterness to his words as though he was finally coming to accept what had happened to them.

He said nothing for a while, deep in thought as though he was trying to work things out in his head. Then at last he said, 'You're right. There's no future for us, because it seems to me that without trust there's nothing at all. I knew I should never have allowed myself to get close to you all over again. I was just setting myself up for heartbreak, wasn't I?'

She turned away from him as Ben came out into the garden once more. Her throat was aching and her eyes burned with unshed tears. She couldn't answer him, and she escaped into the house, her heart pounding, her throat constricted.

She wished she'd never remembered how he'd cheated on her. Then she could have gone on loving him in blissful ignorance instead of having to suffer this awful heartache. More than anything, she wanted to be with him, but how could their relationship ever work out with that awful betrayal hanging over them? How was she even going to cope with working alongside him?

Back in A and E the next day she was busy with her patients and managed for the most part to stay out of Matt's way. At lunchtime she went over to the intensive care unit to look in on Danny and find out how he was doing.

'His intracranial pressure is down,' the nurse told her, 'and we've done another CT scan, which shows everything's going along nicely. There's no sign of the blood clot building up again.'

'So you'll be removing the drainage tube soon?'

'In a day or so, I should think. He's doing really well. We're very pleased with him.'

Saffi was relieved. Danny was sitting up in bed, talking to his parents, and it looked as though his mother was showing him pictures in a story-book. She said cautiously, 'Is there any sign of brain damage?'

The nurse shook her head. 'Thankfully, no. He's a very lucky boy.'

'He is.' Smiling, Saffi went back down to A and E to finish her shift. She was glad Danny was doing so well. Things could have turned out so differently if it hadn't been for Matt's prompt action.

'Shall I help you with the patient in Room Three?'

Gina asked, cutting in on her thoughts. 'It's an infant with a bead lodged in her ear. You might need me to distract her while you try to get it out.'

'Yes, okay. Thanks, Gina.' Saffi frowned. It was an uncomfortable feeling, working with this woman, now that she'd remembered everything that had happened between her and Matt. She had to dredge up every ounce of professionalism she possessed in order to do her job properly, without letting her emotions get in the way.

'Are you all right?' Gina was studying her closely. 'Matt said you were recovering new memories all the time. Has it upset you?'

Saffi closed her eyes briefly. 'It has. It was bound to, don't you think?' She looked at Gina, beautiful, green-eyed, her hair shining with health. Was it any wonder that Matt's head had been turned, especially if Gina had made a play for him?

'There's nothing going on between us, you know,' Gina said quietly. 'I'm engaged to be married—look.' She held out her left hand, showing her sparkling diamond ring.

'Oh, I see.' Saffi's brows drew together. 'Congratulations.' She hesitated. 'That wasn't actually what was bothering me.'

'No.' Gina's voice was flat. 'Matt said you'd remembered me being in his bedroom.' She winced. 'I wanted to get back with him after he'd finished with me, so I went to see him when I knew you were busy at work. He was friendly enough, but he didn't want anything to do with me as a girlfriend and wanted me to leave, so

I said was feeling ill…a bit sick, faint, and so on. I lied to you, Saffi.'

Saffi stared at her, shock holding her still, rooted to the spot. Had she made a terrible mistake?

'I was desperate to make him want me. He said perhaps I should lie down for a while, undo my skirt to ease the pressure on my waist, and I did as he said. Only I undid a few more buttons on my blouse than was necessary. He just drew the curtains and left me alone. After a while, he came to see if I was all right.'

She swallowed hard. 'I wanted him to love me, but he just saw me as a friend. I felt so unhappy, and when you turned up after your shift had ended, I wanted to finish things between you, the way he'd finished things with me. I thought, maybe, if he didn't have you, he might turn to me after all.' She pressed her lips together. 'He never did.'

Saffi let out a long, shuddery breath. 'It was all a lie? All of it?'

Gina nodded. 'I'm sorry. I know what I did was stupid, hurtful. It's just that I was hurting too, inside.'

Saffi's head was reeling. All this time she'd refused to listen to Matt. She'd believed what Gina had said at the time, and she'd sent Matt away. Without trust, he'd said, there was nothing at all. He would never forgive her.

'Saffi, I really am sorry.'

Saffi nodded. It took everything she had to keep going and she said now, 'I'm glad you told me.' She took in several long breaths to steady herself. What was she to do?

She gazed around her without seeing for a moment or two. Then gradually, the sights and sounds of the hospital came back into view and she said dully, 'We'd better go and see what we can do about this bead.'

She made herself go into the room and talk soothingly to the little girl and her mother. 'I'm going to look inside your ear with this,' she said to the two-year-old, showing her the otoscope. 'It won't hurt, I promise.'

When she could see the shiny object, way down in the ear canal, she tried to gently remove it using special forceps, but when that didn't do the trick, she asked Gina for suction equipment. After a few seconds, much to the mother's relief, she'd retrieved the bead.

She left the room a few minutes later, leaving Gina to talk to the patient and her mother and clear away the equipment. The only thing on her mind was to find Matt and talk to him, though how she was going to persuade him to forgive her lack of trust was beyond her right now. He'd seemed to have made up his mind, finally, that there was no point any longer in trying to win her back. He'd decided she wasn't worth the effort.

'He went out on a call,' Jake told her, 'and I think he's going to be tied up in meetings all afternoon. Do you want me to pass on a message?'

'No, that's all right, Jake. Thanks. I'll catch up with him later.'

She arrived home feeling washed out and dreadful. How could she have been so blind, so certain that she'd had things right all this time?

She was pacing the floor of her living room when

Jason turned up at the house, and she groaned inwardly. This was the last thing she needed, but some part of her insisted that even though he would never win her round she should let him say his piece. Wasn't that where she'd gone wrong with Matt, by not listening to him?

They went back into the living room.

'I'm going back to Hampshire tomorrow,' Jason told her.

'So soon? I thought you had another couple of days here?'

'No.' He shook his head. 'I have to go and see the head of a regional pharmacy service. It's a new contact for me, and my bosses didn't want me to miss it.'

She smiled. 'It sounds as though your job is going really well. You must be pleased.'

He shrugged. 'I work hard and make a lot of contacts, but I could have done without that one right now. I need more time here to persuade you that we belong together.'

'It's never going to happen, Jason,' she said, unhappy because she had to hurt him yet again. 'I don't know how it was before, but I can't see how we were ever a couple, to be honest. I don't think I've changed so much from how I was before the accident.' She still felt the same way about Matt as she'd always done, so how could it be any different with Jason? Something had to be wrong somewhere.

'You're being very cruel to me, Saffi. How can you say these things to me?'

She sent him a troubled look. 'I don't mean to be

cruel. I'm trying to be straightforward with you, so that you don't have any illusions as to how it will be.'

'But I love you, and you loved me. How can that all have changed?'

Her expression was sad as she tried to explain, 'I don't think it was ever that way. It feels to me as though you've conjured something up in your mind and made it into something that never was. It's what you want to believe.'

He moved closer to her. 'You're my blonde, beautiful, blue-eyed angel,' he said. 'How could I not love you?'

'It isn't love, Jason. You're infatuated with someone you can't have. Don't you see that?'

'All I see is you and me, together.'

He slid an arm around her and pulled her to him. 'I'm not letting you go, Saffi. You're mine, and sooner or later you'll see that I'm right.'

He tried to kiss her and she pushed him away. 'No, Jason, stop it.'

'It'll all come right, you'll see.' He ignored her protests and backed her up against the wall, clasping her wrists and pinning her there with his body.

'I said no, Jason. Get off me. Let go of me.' She struggled, trying to wriggle free, and as they tussled he somehow knocked over a stool. It fell against the wall with a crash, and it made her realise how determined he was. 'Jason, this is crazy,' she said. 'Let me go.'

He tightened his grasp on her wrist and she stared up at him, frightened, afraid of what he might do. A startling image flashed across her mind, of another place, another time, when he'd grabbed her wrist in that very same way.

'Oh, no…no…' she cried. 'This can't be happening, not again.' The last time he'd held on to her this way they'd been at the top of a flight of stairs. She'd tried to get away from him, and the next thing she'd known she'd been tumbling down and down and then there had just been blackness until she'd woken up in hospital.

'You're the reason I fell down the stairs. You were trying to stop me from breaking up with you.' Her voice was rising with panic. 'Please, Jason. Think about what you're doing. Do you want it to happen all over again? Are you deliberately trying to hurt me?'

He didn't get the chance to answer because all at once there was the sound of a key scraping in a lock, and Matt came rushing into the room through the connecting door.

'Let go of her,' he said in an ominously threatening voice. His jaw was clenched in anger and there was the fierce promise of retribution in his grey eyes.

Jason paled with fright. 'What are you doing here?'

'Never mind that. Do as I said. Let her go.'

Jason hesitated for a few seconds too long, and Matt was on him right away, putting an arm around his neck and yanking him backwards, while at the same time hooking his leg from under him.

Matt gave him a push and Jason fell to the floor. Standing over him, his foot firmly placed over Jason's arm, Matt glanced at Saffi.

'Are you all right?'

Saffi resisted the urge to rub her sore wrists, and nodded. She was winded, breathing hard after the skirmish, and her heart was pounding as she wondered what she would have done if Matt hadn't intervened. Perhaps a knee to the groin would have done the trick?

'Let me up,' Jason said, struggling to get to his feet.

Matt pushed him back down with his other foot. His balance and his strength were incredible, and Saffi realised his sessions at the gym had definitely paid off.

'What do you want me to do with him? Do you want to call the police?' Every time Jason made a move, Matt pushed him down again.

'I don't know,' she said, filled with anxiety. 'Do you think he'll come back and try again?'

'I won't. I won't do that.' Jason's voice shook as he became more desperate.

Matt ignored him. 'I don't think it's very likely,' he said, looking at Saffi. 'If he does, he'll certainly regret it, because I'll do more than drag him off you next time. He'll wish he'd never been born.'

'I just want him out of here,' she said, and Matt nodded.

He grasped Jason by the collar of his sweatshirt and dragged him to his feet. 'You heard what she said. Get out of here, and don't come back.'

He pushed him towards the front door and pulled it open wide. 'Get in your car and don't come within twenty miles of her, don't phone her, don't email, don't write to her. If you try to contact her in any way, we'll get an injunction against you. Are you clear on all that?'

Jason nodded, his face ashen. He must have realised

he didn't stand a chance against Matt, who was so much fitter and stronger than he was. He didn't say another word but hurried over to his car and drove away as though he was terrified Matt would come after him.

'Thank you for coming in and rescuing me,' Saffi said when Matt returned to the living room. 'I thought you would be out all day. I thought I was completely alone with him.' The after-effects of her ordeal suddenly kicked in and she began to tremble. Feeling behind her for a seat, she sank down into the sofa and clasped her hands in her lap.

Matt came to sit beside her. After a moment of hesitation, as he appeared to be at war within himself, he wrapped his arms around her and held her until the trembling stopped. Then he said softly, 'I'll make you a hot, sweet drink. That should help you to feel better.'

She nodded silently. She would have gone after him, but her legs were weak and all the energy had drained out of her. The shock of Jason's assault and the memory of how her fall down the stairs had come about were too much for her to take in. She started to shake all over again.

'Here, drink this.' Matt handed her a cup of tea and helped her to clasp her hands around it. He sat with her as she tried to gain control of herself.

'Thank you for this.' She swallowed some of the reviving tea and then slid the cup down onto the coffee table. 'I can't tell you how glad I am that you came through that door when you did.' She sent him a puzzled look. 'But I don't understand how you were there, how you knew to come to me.'

'I was afraid something like this might happen. Ben told me that you were talking in the garden yesterday. He said Jason was cross when you said you weren't leaving here and he was angry when you asked him to go, and that started warning bells in my head.' He grimaced. 'I cancelled all my meetings so that I could be here, just in case I was needed.'

'You did that, even though I'd been so awful to you?' She clasped his hand, needing that small contact.

'I was already watching out for trouble after you were followed the other night.'

'By the black car?'

He nodded. 'I'm fairly sure it was Jason in the car. He must have thought you were on your own—perhaps the headrests obscured his vision. Did you tell him you were going to the vet's surgery?'

She frowned, thinking about it. 'I don't remember. I was busy and then… Oh, yes…he wanted to take me out and I said I couldn't go with him because I had to take Mitzi to the vet.'

'He must have been waiting there, ready to follow you home.'

'But why would he do that?'

'He's obsessed with you. He must have followed you before. How was your other car damaged in a rear-end collision? Do you have any recollection of it?'

She nodded slowly, covering her face with her hands as the incident came back to her in bits and pieces. Getting herself together after a minute or so, she said, 'It was when I wanted to finish things with him…he took to following me. When I wouldn't stop the car, he drove me off the road.' She looked at Matt. 'He's out of his mind, isn't he? Perhaps we should have called the police after all, or tried to persuade him to get treatment?'

'I doubt the police would do anything without proof. Were there any witnesses?'

She shook her head.

'And when you fell down the stairs?'

'No.' It came out as a whisper, and she began to shake all over again. 'He must have left me there at the foot of the stairs, knowing I needed help. But he did nothing. Apparently, it was Chloe who called for the ambulance when she arrived home from work. I don't know how long I was lying there.'

He put his arms around her and drew her to him, gently stroking her silky hair. 'It's over now, Saffi. He won't trouble you again.' They stayed together that way for some time, and eventually he said softly, 'It looks as though your memory's come back in full force.'

She gave him a tremulous smile. 'It does, doesn't it?' She gazed up at him, her brow puckering. 'But why did I lose it so completely? I can understand partial amnesia because it was a bad head injury, but such a total loss is unusual—people don't often recover their memories after such a loss.'

'There's probably a combination of reasons. The head injury is one, as you say, but your mind could have been shutting out the bad things, all the emotional trauma that you didn't want to face...like your relationship with Jason.'

'And the end of my relationship with you. That has been the worst of all.' She looked at him anxiously, passing her tongue lightly over her dry lips. 'Matt—I spoke to Gina before I left work today. She told me that she'd lied to me.' Her gaze meshed with his. 'I'm so sorry I doubted you. You were right all along—I should have trusted you.'

'We'll have to start again, won't we...and make a pact to always trust one another?'

'Does that mean you forgive me?' She looked at him in wonderment. 'Do we have some kind of a future together?'

He looked into her blue eyes. 'We'd better have a future. I'm not going to lose you again, Saffi. It's been hell on earth for me these last few days...these last few years, even.'

'But you don't believe in long-term relationships, do you? Wasn't that why you finished things with Gina, because you didn't want any kind of commitment?'

'I thought that was the reason at the time. It was what I told myself. But the truth is, Gina and I were never right for one another. She wanted to get serious, but I knew it would never work.'

He hesitated. 'I never looked for commitment. But then I met you, and I could feel myself getting in deeper and deeper, knowing that you were the one woman I could love. But all the time I was afraid that it would go wrong, that it would end the way it always did with people I cared about...my parents, even my sister was lost to me when we ended up in separate foster-homes. I was afraid to love you in case I lost you. And then the very worst happened. You thought I'd cheated on you.'

He drew in a shuddery breath. 'It made me even more wary of getting involved. When I met up with you again, here in Devon, I was so afraid of being hurt all over again. I told myself I needed to keep my distance, but it was too difficult and I ended up not being able to stay away. And after you remembered what had happened with Gina, I was devastated all over again. It was like my worst nightmare. I thought I'd lost you for ever.'

She lifted a hand to his face and stroked his cheek. 'You haven't lost me. I love you, Matt. I think I knew it almost from the first.' She gently drew him towards her until their lips touched, and he gave a ragged groan, kissing her fiercely, with all the longing and desperation that had built up inside him.

'Will you marry me, Saffi?' His voice was husky with need. 'I couldn't bear to lose you again.'

'Yes...yes, I will...' She wrapped her arms around him, loving the way he ran his hands over her body, over every dip and curve. She kissed him because she loved him, because she wanted him, because she needed him to know that she would be his for evermore.

When they at last stopped to gather breath, she said softly, 'Aunt Annie thought we were meant for each other, you know. She knew how much I loved you and she always had faith in you, even when I was floundering. That must be the reason she left you part of the house. She wanted us to be together, and she knew we'd have to find some way of making it work if we both lived here.'

He chuckled. 'Yes, I'd worked that one out. She was right, wasn't she? I know she couldn't have expected it to happen so soon, but her plans were all intact. She didn't leave anything to chance.'

She snuggled into him, nuzzling his neck and planting soft kisses along his throat. 'I love you so much.'

'And I love you, beyond anything. That's why I came to work in Devon. I knew, sooner or later, you would come to visit Annie and I would do everything I could to win you round. I just had to see you again.' He gave a wry smile. 'And then when you turned up and hadn't a clue who I was, I thought maybe here was my chance to get you to love me all over again.'

'Well, you managed that all right.'

'I did, didn't I? That must say something about true love lasting for ever.' He kissed her again. 'Are we too late for a summer wedding, do you think?'

She smiled up at him. 'I shouldn't think so. I'm sure we'll manage to sort something out.'

'That's good…that'll be perfect.' He gently pressured her back into the cushions and eased himself against her, and after that neither of them had any inclination to move apart for a long, long time.

* * * * *

Mills & Boon® Hardback
February 2014

ROMANCE

A Bargain with the Enemy	Carole Mortimer
A Secret Until Now	Kim Lawrence
Shamed in the Sands	Sharon Kendrick
Seduction Never Lies	Sara Craven
When Falcone's World Stops Turning	Abby Green
Securing the Greek's Legacy	Julia James
An Exquisite Challenge	Jennifer Hayward
A Debt Paid in Passion	Dani Collins
The Last Guy She Should Call	Joss Wood
No Time Like Mardi Gras	Kimberly Lang
Daring to Trust the Boss	Susan Meier
Rescued by the Millionaire	Cara Colter
Heiress on the Run	Sophie Pembroke
The Summer They Never Forgot	Kandy Shepherd
Trouble On Her Doorstep	Nina Harrington
Romance For Cynics	Nicola Marsh
Melting the Ice Queen's Heart	Amy Ruttan
Resisting Her Ex's Touch	Amber McKenzie

MEDICAL

Tempted by Dr Morales	Carol Marinelli
The Accidental Romeo	Carol Marinelli
The Honourable Army Doc	Emily Forbes
A Doctor to Remember	Joanna Neil

0114GEN STD HB

Mills & Boon® Large Print
February 2014

ROMANCE

HISTORICAL

MEDICAL

0114 GEN STD LP

Mills & Boon® Hardback
March 2014

ROMANCE

A Prize Beyond Jewels	Carole Mortimer
A Queen for the Taking?	Kate Hewitt
Pretender to the Throne	Maisey Yates
An Exception to His Rule	Lindsay Armstrong
The Sheikh's Last Seduction	Jennie Lucas
Enthralled by Moretti	Cathy Williams
The Woman Sent to Tame Him	Victoria Parker
What a Sicilian Husband Wants	Michelle Smart
Waking Up Pregnant	Mira Lyn Kelly
Holiday with a Stranger	Christy McKellen
The Returning Hero	Soraya Lane
Road Trip With the Eligible Bachelor	Michelle Douglas
Safe in the Tycoon's Arms	Jennifer Faye
Awakened By His Touch	Nikki Logan
The Plus-One Agreement	Charlotte Phillips
For His Eyes Only	Liz Fielding
Uncovering Her Secrets	Amalie Berlin
Unlocking the Doctor's Heart	Susanne Hampton

MEDICAL

Waves of Temptation	Marion Lennox
Risk of a Lifetime	Caroline Anderson
To Play with Fire	Tina Beckett
The Dangers of Dating Dr Carvalho	Tina Beckett

Mills & Boon® Large Print
March 2014

ROMANCE

Million Dollar Christmas Proposal	Lucy Monroe
A Dangerous Solace	Lucy Ellis
The Consequences of That Night	Jennie Lucas
Secrets of a Powerful Man	Chantelle Shaw
Never Gamble with a Caffarelli	Melanie Milburne
Visconti's Forgotten Heir	Elizabeth Power
A Touch of Temptation	Tara Pammi
A Little Bit of Holiday Magic	Melissa McClone
A Cadence Creek Christmas	Donna Alward
His Until Midnight	Nikki Logan
The One She Was Warned About	Shoma Narayanan

HISTORICAL

Rumours that Ruined a Lady	Marguerite Kaye
The Major's Guarded Heart	Isabelle Goddard
Highland Heiress	Margaret Moore
Paying the Viking's Price	Michelle Styles
The Highlander's Dangerous Temptation	Terri Brisbin

MEDICAL

The Wife He Never Forgot	Anne Fraser
The Lone Wolf's Craving	Tina Beckett
Sheltered by Her Top-Notch Boss	Joanna Neil
Re-awakening His Shy Nurse	Annie Claydon
A Child to Heal Their Hearts	Dianne Drake
Safe in His Hands	Amy Ruttan

Discover more romance at

www.millsandboon.co.uk

- ❤ WIN great prizes in our exclusive competitions
- ❤ BUY new titles before they hit the shops
- ❤ BROWSE new books and REVIEW your favourites
- ❤ SAVE on new books with the Mills & Boon® Bookclub™
- ❤ DISCOVER new authors

PLUS, to chat about your favourite reads, get the latest news and find special offers:

- 🄵 Find us on facebook.com/millsandboon
- 🐦 Follow us on twitter.com/millsandboonuk
- ❤ Sign up to our newsletter at millsandboon.co.uk